#Justice4 Justice

SOUMIK CHAKRABORTY

Title : #Justice4Justice
Author : Soumik Chakraborty

Published By
Redgrab books Pvt. Ltd.
942, Mutthiganj, Prayagraj, 211003
www.redgrabbooks.com
contact@redgrabbooks.com

Printed and bound in Manipal Technologies Limited, Manipal, Karnataka
Paperback, First published by Redgrab Books Pvt. Ltd. in 2021
ISBN : 978-93-90944-58-3

Cover design and Typeset in Redgrab Books arts

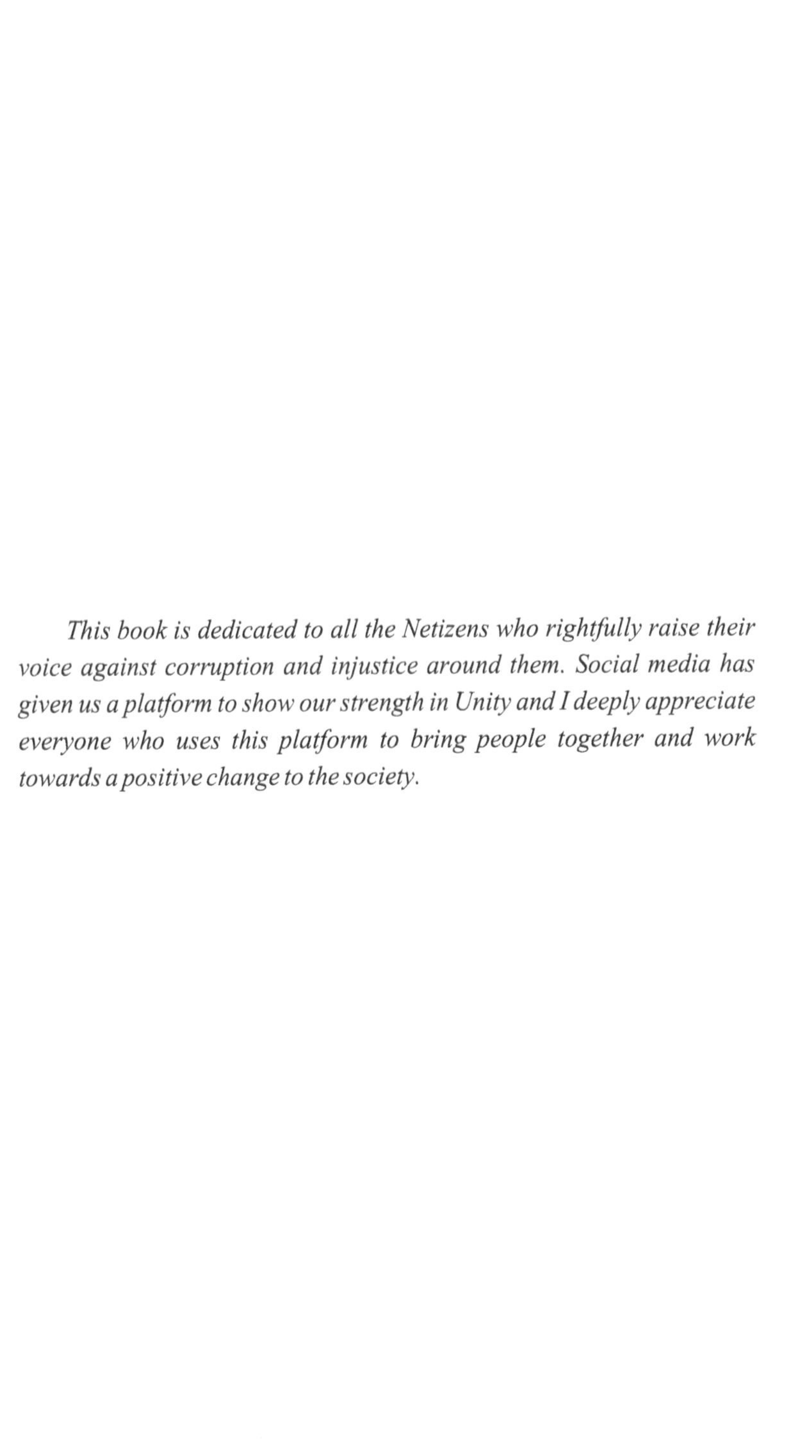

This book is dedicated to all the Netizens who rightfully raise their voice against corruption and injustice around them. Social media has given us a platform to show our strength in Unity and I deeply appreciate everyone who uses this platform to bring people together and work towards a positive change to the society.

ACKNOWLEDGMENTS

I would like to thank my wife Samraggi and my family for their continued support and also all my social media friends who has inspired me with regards to the story line and the social media posts. Special mention to Prachi, my editor and a huge round of applause to Redgrab team, specially Jitendra, for guiding me positively, throughout the publishing journey and helping me out with some great ideas.

CONTENTS

CHAPTER 1

India 4Life

@india4life

Why don't we celebrate 29th February? It comes once every 4 years, just like the World Cup. We celebrate our birthday because it comes once each year, so why can't we celebrate 29th February every Leap Year? #leap year chronicles

#celebratelife

#newcelebrations

00:05 AM · Feb 29, 2020 ·Twitter Web App

89 Retweet **78** Comment **898** Likes

29th February 2020 00:10, Bangalore, Shetty Residence

Mr. Balaram Shetty turned 68 10 minutes ago. It has been years since he retired as a Chief Justice in the Bangalore High Court, but the grandeur hasn't left him yet, and by the looks of it, it will be by his side till his last breath. Even today, his name holds the same honor and prestige in the honorable High Court as it did 7 years ago. He is renowned for multiple traits, including the stringency with which he held the court affairs, his keen instincts which could filter the truth from the Bhagwad Gita-pledged lies but most importantly, his passion for righteousness, and the pride in serving justice.

The 5-ft-6-inch man sulked in his bedroom, alone. His short fingers lighted a match, and his moustache-topped lips tasted the smoke from the pipe. He laid down his thick framed reading glasses and rested his body on the antique bed.

"Where did I go wrong, Srabanti?" he whispered to himself, looking at the picture of his lifeless life partner, hung on the left wall. 15 years ago, Srabanti was diagnosed with cancer. When Mr. Balaram had heard the news about her cancer, he felt his life has been robbed of all its sunshine, and it was only darkness that lay ahead. He hired the best doctors to cure her cancer, and the doctors worked hard to stop the spread of the deadly disease. However, it was always going to be a one-sided race, where Mr. Balaram could not win but only delay the ultimate loss. Unlike his court affairs, here, he could only adjourn the eventuality of this deadly duel for the next three years, till Mrs. Srabanti finally succumbed to the world's most fatal disease.

Mr. Balaram continued talking to his wife, as if she was on the other end of the bed, listening to him patiently, "After you left us, I tried to fill the void and raise our children correctly. I kept them out of harm's way, fulfilled their dreams, got them married, and settled their lives, but this is what I get in return!"

Tears curved its way through the wrinkled skin, but the pain of silence wasn't bearable yet, so he continued talking, "My birthday comes only once every four years. Can you imagine? 4 years! All our children, including Vicky, Ronit, Kuntal, and Pubali, all stay under the same roof with me, in the same house, but they forget even to wish me! And here I was, expecting someone to knock on the door at midnight, so I kept the door open too, so that our seven-year-old grandson, Sparsh, can run to me and hug me. But here I am, brooding alone, on my birthday!"

He took a moment to pause and clear the tears, and then resumed, as if his wife must have been conversant during this pause.

"No, Srabanti, No, they will not wish me tomorrow morning. They know very well that we celebrate my birthday only at midnight, every time, as it comes only on a leap year. They know how passionate I am about my birthdays. I know you will be taking your children's side, but you should know this. They did not grow up as we had dreamed they would. We always wanted them to grow up as good, honest human beings with a good heart, but our love and care has spoilt them. They are just a bunch of brats. None of them value hard work, and they only look for shortcuts in their career. They don't even love or respect me anymore.

"Do you think they stay in this home, together, only for me? Or maybe because of their love for their siblings! No, not at all. None of them can afford to buy their own house, so they stay under this roof. None of them would even blink before leaving this house, if they had the means to do so. All of them are just waiting like hyenas, waiting for me to die, so that they can sell this house to promoters, sell our Kunj Villa, where we shared all our memories."

Another pause and then, "You do not believe me! Do you know how many times they tried to convince me to sell this property to promoters? That is the only issue which brings your beloved siblings to my room. All of them want to settle separately and leave me to die alone. They are only after my properties and wealth, and they do not love me Srabanti, they do not love me."

Mr. Balaram surrendered to tears and buried his head in the pillow. After a few minutes, he woke up from the ashes of his tears, like a phoenix, and the sense of justice kicked in. With red angry eyes, he said, "This cannot go on like this; I have always maintained that justice must be served. And it will be served today; they will have to face justice for how they have treated me."

He dressed up, and, at quarter past midnight, he buzzed a bell to call the servant. Hari responded to the bell and reached Mr. Balaram's room within minutes. Mr. Balaram asked him to wake everyone up and bring them to the drawing room urgently. Hari had his own reservations about his master's words but did not have the audacity to question it, so he left his master's side to call all the other members of the house to the drawing room at the dawn of the night.

CHAPTER 2

Arvind Chatterjee

1h

Bangkok tickets booked, avi toh party suru huyi hain @payalupadhyay @janglibilli @hartelpatel Bangkok vibes, here we come #PartyParty #BangkokDiaries #Travelwithfriends#Mastitravels

48 Likes 12 Comments 1 Share

Finally, the drawing room got crowded on Mr. Balaram's birthday, but there were no cakes. The cheers and birthday wishes were missing and replaced by long yawns. Instead of party wears, all were in sleeping gowns. As usual, the head of the house, Mr. Balaram, sat in the centre reclining chair, whereas his offsprings gathered around him, grumbling amongst themselves about this late gathering. Finally, the oldest of the brothers, Vicky, spoke up.

"What happened, Dad? Hari said it is urgent! All of us thought that you have suddenly become sick, and so we hurried from the midst of our sleep, but you look fine. What's the matter then?""I am sorry to have disappointed your hopes, Vicky, but I am fine, health wise!"

Before Vicky could follow up, Ronit, who was Mr. Balaram's second son, exclaimed, "What do you mean, disappointed? You think we would be happy if you fell ill? What are you saying, Dad? Can you please be a little clearer? You may be retired, but we have office in the morning and do not have time for all this emotional drama in the middle of the night."

Pubali, who was the only daughter of Mr. Balaram, seconded the anger. "Yes, Dad, anything urgent? I have my divorce case hearing tomorrow and need to reach the court quite early."

Mr. Balaram chuckled and said, "Wow, what a noble cause!"

Pubali exclaimed, "Excuse me, Dad! So you want me to continue with an unhappy marriage just because it will suit your public profile?"

Pubali was about to say more, but by then, the youngest brother, Kuntal, stepped in.

"Ahhh, Di, please stop, let's first hear why Dad called us suddenly. The quicker this gets over, the quicker we can go to sleep. Sparsh is sleeping in our room, and we do not want to wake him up with all this chatter!"

Kuntal's wife, Aparajita, the only daughter-in-law of Mr. Balaram, seconded her husband, saying, "Yes, Papa, please tell us, why did you call us at such a late hour?"

Mr. Balaram maintained his composure and said, "All of you are my family. Family is the closest thing to everyone. Your mother and I sacrificed our whole lives for you but do you think all of you have been caring enough towards me, when I am most vulnerable, during my old ages!'

Pubali rubbished the emotion. "Oh, come on Dad, you are going to give us lecture at 1 am in the night? Is this what you called us for? Oh man, you are really getting crazy. Why are all of you oldies like this, such a pain to deal with?"

"Is that any way to talk to your father? Is this what we have taught you?" exclaimed Mr. Balaram.The oldest son took charge. "Pubali, please calm down; let's get this over with and go back to sleep. Dad, please continue, but can you do it a bit quicker, please, considering the wee hour? Please leave the drama from your speech and let's come straight to the point."

Aparajita, the daughter-in-law, again seconded, "Yes, Papa, Sparsh can wake up any moment now. Please be quick."

"Ok, you want it quick? I will be blunt then. I can sense, why all of you stay in this house. It is definitely not to stay with me as none of you has talked to me for five minutes even, for the last few months. None of you want to stay together, live, and laugh with your siblings each day. I know that all of you want to sell this house, take the money, and go your separate ways."

Mr. Balaram paused for a second, but no one disturbed the flow. Few even took their seats. All were attentive now. The sleepy eyes gave way to the most attentive expressions. This was a discussion which all of them were waiting for, and the clock seemed trivial now. Everyone loathed everyone else's greedy, opportunist glances, hardly aware that they themselves were guilty of the same.

"Throughout our life, I and your mother have sacrificed for all of you, to bring you up as best as we can, but I feel I have failed. Unfortunately, none of you grew up as your mother would have wanted. What is the use of staying under the same roof if no one has any warmth for the other?"

A pause again, waiting for someone to resent the charges being pressed, but silence prevailed till Mr. Balaram resumed. "So, I have asked our family lawyer, Mr. Prasad to prepare my legal will. He will bring it to me tomorrow morning for my signatures, but I wanted to brief you about the details myself."

A buzz of excitement caught the wind as everyone straightened and looked at their father with the same expression as a child looks at his father when the father returns from work with a gift in his hand.

"Please note that whatever I am going to say is irreversible and has already been penned down. I primarily have three assets, this house – Kunj Villa, the place which is built up of all your mother's love and memory, the three cars that we have, and my provident fund, which has one crore rupees."

Everyone's eyes gleamed.

"The cars, they are already used by Vicky, Ronit, and Kuntal. As per my will, you can continue to use those cars, even after my death. Only this time, you will own them too."

Pubali rebuked, "But Dad, I do not…"

"I know, darling, you do not use any car; so, to be fair with all of my children, my daughter, Pubali, will receive five lakh rupees more than her brothers."

Pubali calmed down happily, contemplating what car she could buy within five lakhs, whereas her siblings ushered a protest by raising their hands in despair.

Reminiscence of the Ex Chief Justice overseeing his court affairs flared when he disparaged the gestures of protest by sternly knocking his fists on the table. Everyone calmed down.

"After my death, Kunj Villa will be shared into four equal halves among all four of you. You can use it any way you like, but it will not be sold as long as I am breathing. Is that clear?"

A grin flashed through everyone's face, all of them equally excited about the eventuality of Mr. Balaram's death.

"Coming to the 95 lakh rupees in my PF, as I have already allocated five lakh rupees to Pubali for the car, Hari has taken care of this family throughout his life, so I will leave five lakh rupees to Hari."

Ronit interrupted his father and questioned his judgment. "Five lakh rupees for a servant? Are you mad, Dad? Don't you have any sense of responsibility towards us? How can you give five lakh rupees to someone in your will, who is not even bonded by blood. We are your sons, that is our money, and you can't distribute it to just anybody!"

It looked like Mr. Balaram was actually enjoying the anguish in his son's trembling voice. He maintained his composure and showed them exactly how it feels to be on the opposite side. He just said, “I would have loved to discuss this in detail, son, but all of you have important work in the morning, and it is getting too late already. I have taken your advice and trying to finish this as early as possible, so that all of you can go back to sleep. So, please understand that whatever I am saying is already documented and cannot be changed, and let's proceed with further details so that all of you can go back to bed.”

Mr. Balaram took a momentary pause to relish the stunned expression around the table and resumed.

“Now that we have 90 lakhs left, the four of you will each receive five lakhs each after my death, and another ten lakhs will be given to my dearest Sparsh, which has to be used for his schooling and college fees only. Mr. Prasad will release those funds for those purposes only.”

Everyone spoke simultaneously now. “Five lakhs, only five lakhs! Is this a joke? We and Hari will get the same amount! What kind of justice is this father? How can you do this?' The complaints flashed from everyone except Hari.

Mr. Balaram did not speak a single word, but, rather, it seemed like he was cherishing the moment, grinning at everyone's disappointment.

Finally Kuntal calmed everyone down and said, “Dad, what about the rest of the money? There are still 60 lakh rupees left in your PF. Who among us will get that?”

Mr. Balaram was loving every moment of this, and he said, “Oh, that? That won't be in my PF account when I die.”

“What do you mean it will not be there; where will you spend such a big amount?”

“I will spend that amount today, as my birthday gift to myself and your mother.”

Ronit exploded. "How can you spend 60 lakhs on yourself? How can you be so selfish? You are leaving only five lakhs for us and spending 60 lakhs on your birthday? That too at this old age?"

"I have learnt selfishness from all of you, son. All of you have taught me how to forget about your own family and only think about yourself. I have learnt from all of you how to live under the same roof without talking to each other for months. I have learnt from all of you on how to stay meters apart but unaware of even your own family member's health issues. I have learnt all of this from every one of you."

Pubali pitched in desperately. "Dad, you are taking this too seriously. I know you are angry with us and we realize our mistakes too, but you cannot make your will out of anger. Give us some time, and we will surely rectify our faults; we love you and nothing can change that. We will come and talk to you every day. Please believe us."

Mr. Balaram looked up at her daughter with eager eyes, called her over, and blessed her with his hand. He asked her to seat near him, which she obeyed. The ray of hope for love from his children looked to have won him over. He looked up at everyone else and they had an encouraging look, assuring that they will rectify their mistakes too and give their father the time, love and respect he deserved. Then he looked warmly at Pubali and said, "I know you will take care of me, beta, all of you will. I know all of you will come to me every day and talk to me, talk to each other, and there will be happiness in Kunj Villa again. However, I must not forget that all of that will only be a fabricated show, that all of you will enact to enrich your future with my heritage, after my death. So, although I would love for that to happen, I was well prepared for all of your fake promises before I called all of you over. As I said, my will is irreversible, and all of you will receive that much amount only, which will be written in the will. So please, beta, don't shower me with false hopes but rather reflect on what wrong you have done to me in the past few years. You will realize that all of you deserve no better."

While Pubali was left frustrated, and she rushed away from her father and took her former seat, Vicky weaved a new trick, “But where will you spend such a huge amount, Dad? Please let us help you with it; we shall help you with investing the money so that you can get maximum benefits.”

“No, beta, I do not need any help, and it is not an investment.”

Kuntal stepped in. “Not an investment, then what is it! How will you spend 60 lakh rupees?”

“Beta, here is how I will spend it.”

Mr. Balaram brought out a cheque book from his pocket and signed a cheque for 60 lakh rupees as a donation to a cancer research organization.

An awkward silence followed instead of the explosion, which Mr. Balaram had expected. Everyone was too dumbfounded to speak up. Finally, Pubali ushered in her thoughts on this, “Papa, each of us are struggling with our life financially, and in the midst of this, how can you donate such a huge amount to charity?”

“Just the same way, darling, by which, all of you heard that I am spending this money, but none of you heard that I am spending it on my birthday.”

Pubali and others bowed their head in shame for a fraction of second, but Aparajita stepped in. “Papa ji, you cannot do this to all of us just because we forgot your birthday? Is this your love for us? Is this your care for us? How can you leave us with so little?”

“Little! I am leaving all of you with a house, a car, money, and a secured future for Sparsh. Do you think parents will spoon-feed all of you towards success? We can only lay the foundation stone, which and your mother-in-law and I lay long back. Sadly, none of my children is hard working, and they are only looking for shortcuts. If I leave them anything more, that will also get drained away in their luxurious lifestyle but none of them will be able to do any good with it. If one dreams to be rich, they have to do that by their own hard work, not by inheritance."

Vicky said, "Dad, would Mom have wanted this? Would Mom have wanted us to suffer just because we forgot your birthday?"

For the first time in the night, Mr. Balaram stood up and raised his voice, "If you had treated my wife in the way you treat me, I would not have left a single penny for any of you. I am sure she would have wanted the same, if she had seen me suffer because of all of you. I am sure of it. She always believed along with me, Justice should be served, always. If you treat someone poorly, expect the same in return."

"But Dad…"

"Not a word more; I do not want to listen to your nonsense anymore. As I said, all of this is already penned down. Mr. Prasad will read out the rest of the will to all of you. Apologies for wasting your precious sleep. Good Night to all of you."

Mr. Balaram stood up, left his court and made his way towards his bedroom, upstairs. Everyone tried to say something or the other to Mr. Balaram, but they were short of words. Few even spoke up, but Mr. Balaram did not respond or look back and went straight to his bedroom.

CHAPTER 3

Daring Darling

@daredal

If some particular company has not maintained their product quality, I am suing them if I become a father 9 months from now ;)#adulthood #terabhaibaapbansaktahein #greatnight #populationcontrol

08:50 AM · Feb 29, 2020 ·Twitter Web App

267 Retweet **390** Comment **948** Likes

29th February 09:00

Answering to a knock on the door to his room, Kuntal opened it and found his sister, Pubali, on the other side. In any other household, a sister knocking on her brother's door might be common, but not in Kunj Villa, as this had not transpired in the last six months. Kuntal had not even talked to his sister for over three months now. Therefore, she was not exactly someone that Kuntal was expecting, that too, so early in the day. It had been about three months since Pubali had been in her brother's room, but desperate times call for desperate measures. As she was welcomed in, she spared a moment to admire the décor of the room and gave an appreciative look towards the other lady of the house, Aparajita. Kuntal asked her sister, 'Good morning Di, how are you doing!'

"Are you seriously asking this, Kuntal? After last night, how can any of us be happy?"

"I know, Di; even Aparajita was discussing the same thing with me.

How can Dad do this to us? After all, we are the closest ones he has, and technically, we should automatically inherit everything. Why is he doing this to us? Just because we forgot his damn birthday? All those years of lunacy that he has overseen in the courtroom has really screwed his brains!"

"Yes, I know, Kuntal, and that is why we have to go and talk to Papa before Mr. Prasad is here with the will. Before everything becomes legal, we have to win him over, emotionally, and then, convince him to override this will. Firstly, we cannot let that cheque of 60 lakhs leave the house. If that money gets donated to any NGO, there will be no use of softening him up anymore."

"Didi, yes, you are right but did you talk to Vicky and Ronit Bhaiya? Our Dad is a tough nut to crack emotionally. The last 40 years have made him fanatically fall in love with justice, and emotions scarcely get the better of him. So, it's going to take all of us to convince him. We can use Sparsh too; he will surely soften down for his grandson, if not for us."

Aparajita intervened, "No, Sparsh will not be involved in this, as I do not want him to listen to any harsh words that Papa might say."

Kuntal reasoned with his wife. "But darling, that's the whole point; Dad cannot say anything rash in front of Sparsh. I am doing this for his future only. He would benefit most out of it; otherwise, his future is ruined."

While Aparajita pondered what her stand would be, Pubali said, "Yes that's a good plan. Sparsh will definitely be a great help to set the emotional tone and to keep it that way. However, I cannot find Vicky Bhaiya anywhere. Hari told that Vicky Bhaiya had left early morning for jogging. I didn't know he was a jogger, and how can he jog after yesterday night? I wonder where the fuck he is now."

"Maybe he went to get a cake for Papa? But if that happens..." Kuntal was thinking out loud when Pubali spoke aloud, exactly what Kuntal was thinking.

"If he impresses Papa, then he will get the lion's share of the property."

"Exactly, we must not let anyone do anything on his own. We are in this together, and we cannot let anyone make individual moves. Instead of focusing on a personal lion's share, we need to work together to cancel that cheque."

"Yes brother, I agree, but I don't think Vicky Bhaiya is playing by that rule."

"We have to talk sense to him; let's go and discuss it with Ronit Bhaiya. Have you discussed with him already, Didi?"

"No, I knocked on your door first, as you are on my floor. Let's go upstairs and talk to Ronit Bhaiya about this. We need to do something quickly before Mr. Prasad comes over."

Both of them went upstairs to Ronit's room, but he was still sleeping. From the leftovers, clearly, Ronit had smoked some weed last night and was sound asleep. When verbal, loud pitched efforts failed, the siblings shook him up awake. With sleepy, red eyes, Rohit yawned his way out of slumber and stretched his arms to come back to reality. He rubbed his eyes to ascertain the unlikely presence of his brother and sister in the room and asked them, "What are you two up to?"

Kuntal spoke first, "Bhaiya, how can you sleep after last night? We are going to be bankrupt if Dad's will is announced. We need to quickly talk some sense into Dad, otherwise, we will lose our 60 lakhs. We cannot let that happen. We are his children, and he has some duty towards us. I am sure he will agree if we can show some love and affection towards him, talk sweetly to him, respect him, and give him some time. I am sure we can win him over within two days. I will ask Sparsh to spend most of his time with his grand dad, and that will soften him more."

Before Ronit could respond, Pubali spoke up, "But we don't have two days, because Mr. Prasad will come today with the will."

60 lakhs were at stake, so Ronit did not take much time to come back to his senses, and he joined the conversation. “We will have to stop Mr. Prasad from coming today, and even if he does and announces the will, it can be changed any time by Dad, if we win him over. Yes, we have to show a lot of love and unity to him and also we have to show a lot of bonding among us.”

The blatant phoniness of the plan was out, but no one was judgmental about it, as there were larger things at stake.

Pubali said, “Yes I think that should work, lets plan a surprise birthday party today. Let's arrange for some cakes and call some relatives over.”

“But what if Vicky Bhaiya brings the cake now?”

Ronit could not make much sense out of it, and so he questioned, “Why would Vicky Bhaiya bring a cake?”

Pubali briefed him about Vicky's absence and their theory.

“If Vicky goes solo, that would be a problem. We have to do this together. Let's talk to him when he is back, but where will he get a birthday cake at 9 am in the morning?”

Pubali asked, “Should we wait for him, or should we do anything about it?”

At this point of time, suddenly, someone knocked on the door. As their surprised gazes fell on Aparajita at the door, everyone looked at Kuntal with expressive, questioning eyes. Kuntal just shrugged and, like a game of tag, looked at his wife with the same expressive and questioning eyes. Aparajita dashed into the room and said, “What are you guys looking at me for? I am not going to leave my future into the hands of you or my husband. I am going to fight for it, just like all of you. Papa has some responsibility towards me too.”

They were not expecting Aparajita in a sibling's master plan, but this was no moment to be choosy. Aparajita didn't wait to be accepted and said, “The best way to any man's heart is food. Let's cook some good breakfast and lunch for Papa. That should be a good start.”

Her husband approved the idea, but more importantly, others followed. They agreed that it is a good move to start with and quickly made their way downstairs to the kitchen. Hari was brewing the morning tea for everyone and was shocked to see the sudden crowd in the kitchen. The daughter in law of the house took charge. “Hari kaka, leave the kitchen to us; we will prepare breakfast for Papa and everyone else.”

Hari could easily guess the reason for such generosity and said, “Thik hai, Bhabhi, should I finish making the tea for all of you?”

While Hari served tea to all of them, Pubali and Aparajita started discussing on what would be the apt menu for the breakfast when the oldest brother Vicky walked in from the main door, in his joggers, empty handed.

“Bhaiya, where did you go? Come here quickly, we have to discuss something.”

As they discussed their plans with Vicky, he said, “But I don't think Papa will agree; he is a stubborn man, and he looked very pissed off yesterday.”

The youngest brother said, “Bhaiya, he is a father, and he has to forgive us, as it is in their nature. He will forgive us, but we have to do it quickly so that the will does not become official, and we have to stop that cheque somehow. But where were you, Bhaiya? Do you go jogging every day?”

Vicky expressed his seniority by bashing his younger brother, “With 60 lakhs at stake, you are still interested in my jogging? You are right, we have to stop the cheque from being deposited or handed over to the NGO. If that happens, we are screwed; let's quickly make breakfast so that we can talk to Dad about it.”

It was fifteen minutes past 10 when the Masala Dosa and Sambar was ready for breakfast. They quickly asked Hari, "Has Dad woken up? Did he ask about any of us when you gave him tea?"

"Don't know, Mem Saab, Sirji did not open the door when I went to give him tea."

"What do you mean? Dad never locks his door while sleeping; you could have just gone in and woke him up! Ok, give the tea; we will give it along with the breakfast."

"Nahin, Mem Saab, the door is locked from inside. I think he is sleeping."

"Locked from inside? It's 10 am already, and Dad wakes up by 8 am every day."

Aparajita said, "He must have had a disturbed sleep yesterday after what happened at night; even I could not sleep. Let's go and wake him up."

All the siblings and the daughter-in-law made their way upstairs to serve the breakfast in bed. They knocked at their father's door, but no response came from the other side. They knocked for two more minutes, but still no response. Each of them looked at each other. They placed the breakfast on the floor and started knocking heavily. The knocking turned into banging but still no response. They were doing this for 10 minutes now without any response. As time passed, negative thoughts clouded their minds. Could the late night drama have taken a toll on their father's health? Hari joined the chaos, but still no response came from the other side.

Vicky said, "I have a bad feeling about this. Dad has never spoken to us like he did yesterday night. It must have been very painful for him too. I now fear for the worse. Why isn't he responding?"

Ronit suggested, "I think we should break the door, because if anything is wrong, every second is crucial."

All brothers agreed and attempted to break the door, which split open with a loud thud on the third attempt.

Pubali went in first, and within seconds, screamed, ran out of the room, and started crying. Others looked at Pubali first and, with a beating heart, went inside the room. All of them exclaimed all together at the sight of Mr. Balaram's lifeless body lying in the blood-soaked bed.

CHAPTER 4

ArpitaTalukdar

♡ ◯ ∇ ⊓

467 likes

ArpitaTalukdar Bright sunny day. Shooting the mandatory selfie. Coming your way in the next few minutes. #sunnymornings #queen #selfietime

View all 17 comments

5 MINUTES AGO

29th February 10:30 am

Mr. Dhole, the officer-in-charge at the nearest police station, answered Vicky's call. Vicky was so shocked that he could hardly frame words over the phone call, leave alone making sentences that would make sense to the police officer. However, Mr. Dhole already had immense experience in working with saddened and grief-stricken relatives, and he did not need words from Vicky to sense the gravity of the situation. He only urged Vicky for their address. When Vicky said the address, Mr. Dhole said, "I know it may sound rude, but I have to ask this. Is someone's life in danger, or is someone dead?"After a moment of silence, Vicky took a heavy breath and said, 'My father is dead, and there is blood everywhere. Please help." Mr. Dhole assured of his arrival in 15 minutes and that his team would take care of everything. Before dropping the call, he ordered Vicky to ensure that no one touched anything in the room.

As Mr. Dhole and his team of forensic agents reached Kunj Villa, the siblings were gathered at the ground floor, traumatized and wretched. Vicky stepped forward, introduced himself, and confirmed that he has ensured that no one in the house touched anything as instructed. He accompanied them up the stairs to Mr. Balaram's room, meanwhile, explaining how they broke the door open and found their father's lifeless body, with blood oozing from what looked like to be a stab wound.

Mr. Dhole knew the criticality of this murder investigation as soon as he realized that the deceased was the former Chief Justice of the Indian High Court. Normally, CRITICAL wasn't his game. He could foresee the media exposure and constant hierarchical push from the Police Commissioner to resolve such a critical case in a time-bound fashion, and it immediately dissuaded him. Still, in front of an audience, the 44-year-old, 86-kg, and 5ft-5 inch mustachioed rotund police officer could not shy away from his duties. He ordered his team to follow standard protocol and asked the nitty-gritties from everyone in the house, meanwhile, sniffing for a chance to get out from the crowd and escalate this matter, so that a senior officer could be assigned to the case. As soon as he had surveyed the corpse, searched the room for basic evidences, and confirmed that no one of the family has sabotaged the room, Mr. Dhole left the room and called the Police Commissioner.

The Police Commissioner knew well about the sluggish and lethargic approach of Mr. Dhole and that he liked his duties to follow at his own pace and hated timeliness in activities. He was not as intuitive and instinctual as was preferred in his profession. The Police Commissioner also knew that Mr. Dhole often came up with naive and witless judgments, for which his fellow mates humiliate him. He was timid and forgetful and was reluctant to take up vital duties. He could also be easily muffled down or commanded by any strong voice, no matter if it was a police officer or a common citizen. Therefore, the commissioner responded, “Wait, I will assign Rajiv to the case; he should be there within the next hour. You please see to it that no one leaves the house and the murder scene is not damaged. I will see where Rajiv is and inform him."

"You mean Superintendent of Police Rajiv Bakshi, sir?"

"Yes. Have you worked with him previously?"

"Yes, in the Green Man serial killer case, sir."

"Oh! That's one of Rajiv's masterpieces, so you already know how he works. Please co-operate with him. This case will get a lot of media attention, and we need to solve this as soon as possible."

"Yes, sir, sure."

"Do you have any doubts about anyone in the family?"

"Not yet, sir; I have not discussed with them."

"Then what the fuck are you doing there Mr. Dhole...useless?"

"Sure sir. Yes, sir. I will interview them straight away, sir."

"No need, I would rather have Rajiv do that; you just wait for him there."

"Sure, sir."

The call hung up, but before that, Mr. Dhole had to hear 'a bunch of assholes' as a parting speech.

CHAPTER 5

India 4Life

@india4life

BREAKING NEWS! Former Chief Justice Balaram Shetty found dead in his room, with stab wounds. May his soul RIP @BangalorePolice you need to appoint your best officer to this case.

#greatsoul #chiefjusticeneedsjustice #RIP #saddemise

10:56 AM · Feb 29, 2020 ·Twitter Web App

53 Retweet **23** Comment **2** Likes

Arvind Chatterjee

12 m

So sad to hear about the death of Former Chief Justice Balaram Shetty. He was a true jewel of the nation. #RIPSir #findthecriminal #depressed

1 Likes 56 Comments

He already held a sniper in his hand and now needed to find a vantage point, so that he could make good use of it. He scoped nearby buildings and zeroed in on one having wooden windows with broken glasses. This was a war zone, so broken glass windows were a common site and would not arouse suspicion. It took him two minutes to reach the window and a further two minutes to set up his sniper. The art was staying invisible and wait for the right moment. After staying still for 5 minutes, the car with the two hostages came into view. It was around 500 meters away from him. He had to make a decision and that too, fast. Should he shoot now or should he scope the car till it comes to a halt at the recon site. However, surely there will be more hostiles to deal with in the latter option, other than the four in the car already. The hostages were distinguishable as they had blindfolds. By instinct, he chose hastily and fired a shot at the armed man at the rear of the open hooded car. The bullet hit his right arm, but the power of the sniper dropped him overboard from the moving car. One less guy to deal with, and that's what mattered. The driver was an easy target, but he was the most harmless one as it's hard to shoot a gun while driving in a shootout battle. The other two goons bellowed at the sudden bullet shot and looked around for the origin of it. The driver notched up a gear, and the car's tyres screeched for speed. He took his next shot at the goon at the front seat, but he missed. To make matters worse, this shot gave away his location. He reloaded his sniper and was about to take another try but ducked as the window was by now hammered by counter bullets. He had no time to hide; they could kill the hostages any moment now. He rose up again, aimed, and fired, all within a fraction of a second.Bull's eye, this time he got the front seat goon, but in this process, he had taken a bullet in the shoulder. His vision turned red. He could have used a medipack, but he did not have time. The gunshots towards him had stopped, which could only mean that they were pointed towards the hostages now. He had a terrible pain in his right shoulder, and the sniper was too heavy. Still, he gathered all his strength and put it back up in the window. The goon was indeed pointing the gun at the hostages and would shoot any moment now. He did not have time to aim, and he fired. It missed, but it disarranged the goon. He quickly reloaded his sniper and was about to shoot again when his wife called from the other room.

He did not respond to the first call and took his shot. This time, head shot. Now, the driver was the only one standing between him and the mission. He aimed at the driver and was about to take the shot when his wife slammed the door and entered the room. He had to look back at her, but by then, the driver had killed both the hostages. Mission Failed.

Rajiv irritably dropped the Xbox controllers and said, "Can't you wait for 10 minutes, Devika? I am stuck at this mission for two days and was about to complete it, but you rammed in. What is it?"

"You and your Xbox. Is there any dearth of violence in your work life that you have to kill others in your games too? I am calling you for so long and you are playing video games in this garage, which is your stupid man cave. Why did I allow you to buy these video games? Every day you go out, I am left here, worrying sick, whether you are going to return home safely, and how do you repay me! By shouting at me!"

Rajiv knew that there was no way he could win this argument and so, he conceded defeat. "Ok, I understand, but why were you calling me? I thought you were busy with your kitty party, and 'mankind' isn't allowed there."

Rajiv's wife Devika said, "Yes, that's true, but we need your help urgently. Please come. Quickly, it's serious."

Rajiv was clueless about what he was getting into, but the grim prospect of solving problems of a bunch of his wife's friends did not light him up. He entered the ladies' room with a grumpy face. Apart from his wife and his darling daughter Saloni, seven other women were there, who were the members of his wife's kitty party. Rajiv did know them by name as his wife keeps talking about them but he could not match those names to any of the faces in the room. This was the first time he was invited to their kitty party. Everyone smiled at Rajiv and welcomed him. Rajiv felt awkward and took a seat. Saloni left her seat and smilingly sat on the handle of the sofa on which her father was seated. She was a Daddy's girl. Rajiv waited for someone to speak up and clear the awkward silence. That is what kids are for. Saloni excitedly explained to her father "Dad, you know what happened?"

Rajiv playfully said, "No, my darling," and smiled.

Saloni punched her Dad's shoulders and exclaimed, "Someone stole a gold necklace from Romila aunty's bedroom. We need your help to find it, Dad."

Rajiv did not know who Mrs. Romila was and looked around for someone to help identify her. Mrs. Romila must have noticed it as she adjusted her posture on the sofa and initiated the conversation, "Rajiv Ji, we have heard so much about you, and we are so proud of you. A year back, when you solved the Green Man's case, you were on every news channel. I used to tell everyone that this is Devika's husband. Presently, I am in a big problem, so can you please help me out? Someone has stolen a gold necklace from my bedroom."

Rajiv too adjusted his position in the sofa and sat straight. "Thanks a lot, but, how much was it worth, how did it look like, and when did it get stolen?"

"It was worth 5 lakhs. It was for my daughter's wedding. I got a picture of it here." She unlocked her phone and gave it to Rajiv. "Please, have a look."

Rajiv looked at the picture. It was Mrs Romila, wearing the necklace. The necklace looked beautiful. It had a blue engraved stone as the main attraction in the centre and elegant crafting to cover the rest. Like any other husband, Rajiv could not fathom why the piece of jewelry would cost a fortune, but he deemed that question unnecessary and irrelevant now.

Mr. Romila continued, "My daughter, Pari, lives in Calcutta. She works in an IT firm there. The last time she came home, I had shown her the necklace. She did not like it, as the style was out of fashion. She surfed the internet and showed me a new style from the internet, which closely resembled the old one. She asked me if the necklace could be molded to the new style. I showed it to our local goldsmith, and they changed it to this style, which you see in the picture. I wore it and sent it to my daughter to show her the necklace with the style she wanted."

"How long ago was this?"

"Around a week back."

"And do you have any suspicion as to who could have done this?"

"Apart from my husband and me, we have two servants, and they leave our house by 6 pm every day. Aside from them, the only other person I can suspect is my maternal aunt. She came to our house for two days, and the necklace has been missing since then. However, she is 68 years old, which makes me feel guilty to doubt on her."

"Did you complain to the local PS?"

"No, I thought that I misplaced it, and I searched for it till today morning. I am wondering if you can help me with it. I cannot afford to lose it. My mother-in-law gave it to me, and it's a tradition to pass it on to the next generation. Please help me. It is priceless to me, and it is costly too. I do not have that kind of money to make Pari a new one, and it holds a lot of emotional value."

Saloni nudged her father. To her, her father was a miracle man. He could do anything. "Papa, please help Romila aunty."

Rajiv had already melted to his daughter's cute expressions and earnest request. On top of that, Devika also nudged Rajiv to help her friend. Soon, the symphony spread, and every lady in the room requested Rajiv to help their friend. Rajiv shyly said, "Of course, I will help you, but you will have to lodge a formal complaint. Then only I can get it moving. Can you please send me the picture to my Whatsapp, and can you please tell me which your local PS is?"

Mrs. Romila asked for Rajiv's phone number, immediately sent the photo to him, and informed him about her PS. Rajiv could have done the next steps in privacy, but he had all the attention of the room, and everyone expected to see some heroic actions. Rajiv would never shy away from a chance to be the protagonist, especially in front of his wife and her daughter. Whereas the former thought of him as useless, the latter thought of him as a Superman. He forwarded the photo to a Whatsapp group, called a police officer, and dictated, "I have sent the photo of a gold necklace. Tell our thieves and black market network that Rajiv Bakshi has a special interest in this stolen gold necklace, and if I do not get it back within tomorrow, Rajiv Bakshi is coming after every one of them. Is that clear?"

As Rajiv dropped the phone, Devika shrugged her head and thought to herself what a show-off her husband was. However, she loved it that every one of her friends was impressed with Rajiv's self-confidence and authority. Rajiv looked up to Mrs. Romila and said, "Please don't worry; you will get it back by tomorrow evening." Saloni raised her hands up in the air and cheered for her father. She was delighted and hugged her Dad tight. Everyone else thanked Rajiv for the assurance, and when Saloni hugged her father, everyone clapped with joy.

Next day, in the afternoon, Rajiv called Mrs. Romila and confirmed that the necklace would be delivered anonymously to her doors. In addition, he advised her to use a new goldsmith henceforth, dismiss the existing laundryman, and get a new one.

When Mrs. Romila received the necklace from an anonymous post at her home, she could not stop singing praise of Rajiv in Devika's kitty party Whatsapp group. Everyone discussed about the confidence with which Rajiv had promised and how he had delivered on that promise in less than 24 hours. When anyone's husband does something exemplary, the other woman's husbands take a hit. All women complained about their lazy and useless husbands, and how lucky Devika was to have such a heroic husband. They sang Rajiv's praise so much that even Devika was compelled to think for a minute that her husband wasn't that much useless after all, and maybe there was a slight chance that he was indeed a hero, as her daughter thought. However, when she yelled for Rajiv to tell him about it, Rajiv did not respond. She searched for Rajiv in every room and finally found him playing Xbox in his man cave, again. The bubble of heroism burst, and Rajiv was back as a useless husband, again. Like any other wife, she cursed her fortune to be married to the most lazy and irritating person in the world.

Next day morning, during breakfast, Rajiv received the call from the Police Commissioner and heard about the sad demise of Mr. Balaram Shetty. The Commissioner urged him to take up the case and solve it as quickly as possible. Without knowing a single detail about the case, he confidently confirmed that he would solve the case within a week. As Rajiv dropped the phone and relayed the details about the phone call to the two ladies at the breakfast table, their reaction were as opposite as the two sides of the same coin. The younger one hooted in happiness that her hero was going to bring more criminals to justice, whereas the older one looked angry. She silently kept blabbering some incoherent words around the meaningless promise Rajiv made, without even knowing the ABCs of the case. Rajiv and Saloni looked at each other, high fived, and started laughing at Devika's reaction, but Rajiv did not have a clue then what a mess he was getting into.

CHAPTER 6

ArpitaTalukdar

♡ ▢ ▽ ⌑

3 likes

ArpitaTalukdar Heartbroken to hear about the death of Justice Balaram Shetty. A true son of India

#RIP #Justicewillbeserved #Evilwillbepunished

View all 67 comments

16 MINUTES AGO

Rajiv Mehta was the Superintendent of Police in Bangalore, and he was one of the most competent police officers in his department. He held countless awards and medals for his achievements in apprehending multiple high profile criminals and hence could establish a strong resume for himself in his career path. Unlike his fellow colleagues, he was honest, instinctive, insightful, and exceptionally intelligent. His height of 5ft 2 inches did not give him the edge in physical activities and combat. Therefore, he relied more upon his brains than muscles. At the age of 52, he still carried his innocence in his clean-shaven face, the kind of face which gave you comfort, did not scare you, and did not let you realize his supremacy of intellect and his achievements. The most distinct feature about him was his blue eyes. It reflected his biggest strength to not miss out any minute detail from the crime scene and extract out criminals from the mass. He was also a responsible person and passionate about his family, specially his daughter, Saloni, who was in the tenth standard now. Rajiv was interrogative with his investigation. He would raise multiple questions until he was satisfied with the findings. He was also remorseless towards criminals but very much committed towards the righteous sentiment of working 'for' the citizens; hence, he valued every citizen's emotions.

As he stepped in Kunj Villa, with his aviator glasses, every one of the Shetty family members knew immediately that he would be the investigating officer and not the short, fat police officer who was busy with a cup of tea. Mr. Dhole dropped his glass of tea and timidly went towards Rajiv. “Sir, it's been a year since we met for the Green Man case. How have you been? You look much fitter than last time, sir.”

“Did you have to bring the topic of fitness up, Mr. Dhole? I would have no other choice but to criticize you on that; so, let's start with another topic. Tell me about the crime scene quickly, and we will complete our chit chat later.”

“This case is about the murder of former Justice Balaram Shetty. He retired seven years ago as the Chief Judge of Bangalore High Court.”

“Are we sure that it's murder?”

“Yes, sir; he was stabbed with a sharp object, must have been a knife, and he bled to death.”

“Did you find the murder weapon?”

“No, sir, the murder weapon could not be found, but the stab wounds are clearly visible.”

“Ok, who discovered the body?”

“The whole family discovered it, together. It was Mr. Balaram Shetty's birthday today. The children planned to make breakfast for their, father but when they went with it, Mr. Balaram's door was locked from inside. As he was not responding, they broke the door and found the dead body."

"And did any of them tamper with the evidence in the room?"

"Everyone has said that no one went near the corpse and they immediately called the police."

"When was Mr. Balaram last seen alive?"

"All the family members last met with their father yesterday morning, during breakfast. However, the servant served dinner to Mr. Balaram around 10 pm. After that, no one saw him till his lifeless body was discovered in the morning."

"So, no one went to wish him at midnight? No one saw him after midnight, on his birthday."

"No, sir, all of them said that they last saw their father yesterday, during breakfast."

"Okay, have you searched the room?"

"No, the Police Commissioner asked me to wait for you."

"No, Mr. Dhole. The Commissioner told me that he had stopped you from interrogating others, but he did not stop you from searching for clues."

"Oh, sir, maybe I misunderstood."

"No, Mr. Dhole, you understood it correctly but did not bother to put your lethargic, useless ass to some actual work. At least add some value to your time, Mr. Dhole. If I see one more incidence of slacking from you, I warn you, I will see to it that you are back to being a havildar. Is that clear?"

"I mean, I mean, sir…"

"Is that clear or not?"

"Yes, sir, clear; you will find nothing to complain about anymore."

"Fine, I will go and investigate the crime scene, and then we will talk to the family members."

"Sure, sir, let's go."

"You do not need to go; you have a far more important work to do. Give me a background check on every member of the household, including the servant. I want it within the next hour, before we talk to them."

"Ok, sir, *ho jayega*, sir."

CHAPTER 7

Daring Darling

@daredal

India lost one of its knights. RIP Justice Balaram Shetty @BangalorePolice act fast to catch the murderer so that his soul may rest in peace. #nohastagforgrief #sadme #ilovedhim

11:24 AM · Feb 29, 2020 ·Twitter Web App

45 Retweet **22** Comment **3** Likes

Rajiv had a good look at the house first. When he had entered through the main gate of the property, there laid two small gardens on either side of the pathway that he walked through, towards the building, Kunj Villa, as they had named it. Once inside Kunj Villa, he entered a drawing room. On the right hand side was the kitchen, servants' room, and a common bathroom. On the left hand side of the drawing room, there were two large en suite rooms, divided by a staircase in between which led to the first floor. These two bedrooms in the ground floor were of Mr. Kuntal Shetty, the youngest brother and Mrs. Pubali Shetty, the only daughter of the deceased.

As he moved up the stairs, to his right hand was a dead end, which gave way to the doors of Mr. Vicky Shetty's room, the eldest son. To his left, straight ahead, was the room of the deceased. The corridor of the first floor moved left from Mr. Balaram's room to end in Mr. Ronit Shetty's room. Each bedroom except the servants' had its own bathroom attached to it, so there were no common bathrooms apart from the one which was used by the servant only. Once Rajiv had explored the structure of Kunj Villa, he went inside Mr. Balaram's room. All the house members followed him in, but he asked all of them to leave and go to their own room except the servant. Rajiv kept Hari by his side to be briefed about how they discovered the body.

On his way inside, Rajiv whispered to Hari, “Is there anyone you suspect in the family, who could have killed your beloved master?”

Hari bit his tongue and vehemently shook his head in denial. “Never, sir, none of them could have committed such a brutal murder.”

Rajiv further questioned if Hari had his doubts on anyone outside the house.

Hari answered “For the last week, I have seen a lady outside the main gate, staring for hours at Kunj Villa. She looked poor. My deceased master saw her too, and, on his advice, I went to the gates to question her intentions. I thought she would flee when she would see me approaching, but the woman stood her ground. When I questioned her, she replied that it is none of my business. She is in the main street, and she can do whatever she likes. She began to squabble with me, so I quickly rushed inside, closing the gates. When I told this to my master the day before yesterday, he had advised me to get something to cover the gates, so that no one can peak inside. I arranged for it, but before that, my master left us.” Hari ended the sentence, sobbing. Rajiv patted on his shoulders and urged him inside the room. As Rajiv entered the room, there were three police officers surveying the area and a photographer taking photos. He asked one of them to discuss with Hari about the suspicious woman outside Kunj Villa and get a sketch made.

He had a quick look around the room. The main charm was the antique bed in the middle of the room, a magnificent piece of work. In a sharp contrast, its magnificence was invalidated with what it held—the blood soaked body of Mr. Balaram. To the opposite of the entrance door was the bathroom. There were two transom windows in the room, but the opening was too small for anyone to come in or go out that way. On the wall along the main door, there was a sofa, followed by an antique drawer with a big mirror. There were two decorative items on the opposite wall, along which the two windows lay handsomely. Apart from this, there was a closet to the right side of the bed, and parallel to it, on the left, there was a 4x4 shelf, used as a library, which hosted a hefty number of books. Moreover, the final attraction of the room, an antique locker chest, mounted on a table. The chest was on the diagonally opposite corner of the main door. Therefore, if someone needed to reach the chest, he would have to cross the vigilant eyes of the former Judge, lying in his bed. There were no other exits in the room apart from the main door.

"Hari? Are you sure that this main door was locked when the family found the body?"

"Haan, saab."

"Locked as in bolted from inside or locked by a key which can be operated from outside?"

'Sir, there are no keys for the door; it has to be locked from the inside, using this door latch at the top of the door. I will show you."

Hari demonstrated how the door could be locked from the inside. There were two panels to the door. Hari closed both of them. The right panel had a latch, attached to the top left hand corner, the part where the two panels met. Hari operated the latch to lock the door, by moving it upwards, into the bolt, attached to the wooden doorframe.

Rajiv questioned, "So, only your Saab could have locked the door from inside?"

"Haan, Saab, this door cannot be locked from outside."

"Does Saab always lock the door from inside?"

'Never, sir. Saab often called me in the middle of the night for help by ringing the bell by the side of his bed; so he never locked the door. We were all surprised when we saw the doors locked."

"Then how can a killer come and escape? If the doors were locked from inside, how could he have escaped? There are no other ways out."

"Nehi pata, sir."

At that moment, an officer approached Rajiv and said, "Through the bathroom, sir; the ventilator fan is missing. It is a small space to come in or go out, and it would take an athletic person to reach it. However, that is the only way someone could have left the room."

"Is it? Let's go and check that out first."

Rajiv inspected the bathroom. The open round space for the ventilator fan was right above the commode, about six feet from it.

Rajiv turned to Hari, "Where is the ventilator fan?"

"Saab, it was not working, and so the carpenter took it for repairs."

"When was it?"

"Yesterday morning, sir."

"And from when was it not working?"

"For about two weeks, sir."

"And who called the carpenter?"

"Kuntal Babu, sir."

Rajiv looked for the fittest police officer among the three and zeroed in on Mr. Dutta. He asked him to climb up to the ventilator by stepping on the commode. Mr. Dutta was astounded, but the stern tone of Rajiv and his seniority could not be questioned. Therefore, he cautiously leapt on the commode and stretched upwards to reach the gap in the ventilator. His hands could hardly reach it but still, the uphill task of pulling his body up took three tries. Finally he could squeeze in, somehow, on to the gap in the ventilator. If he were a few centimeters rounder, he would not fit in. A third of his body was hanging out of the outer wall, and the rest of it was visible to Rajiv. Mr. Dutta expected orders to come down, but Rajiv said, “Mr. Dutta, can you see any pipes around you which you can use to climb down?”

“Yes, sir, it is there to my right.”

“Can you grab it?”

“Yes, sir.”

“Fine, then please grab it and try to climb down the pipe.”

Everyone including Hari was shocked and looked at Rajiv. One can only imagine what would be going through Mr. Dutta's mind at that moment. Half of his body hanging out through the ventilator, he said, “It's too risky, sir. I may fall down, or the pipe may break.”

“Ok, come back in; thanks Mr. Dutta.”

Five minutes later, an exhausted Mr. Dutta touched the ground and heaved a sigh of relief.

Rajiv patted Mr. Dutta's shoulder and said, “As per your recent experience, what do you think would the murderer's physicality be like?”

Mr. Dutta replied, “He must be more than 6 feet tall, slim, and athletic.”

Rajiv turned towards Hari and took a good look at him. He would be around 5 feet 9 inches tall, but he was fit and healthy. His age of around 64, however, discouraged further ideas in Rajiv's mind.

Rajiv asked Hari, “Does anyone in the house fit this description?”

“I do not know if I should say this, but obviously, you must have noticed that Saab's youngest son, Kuntal is tall and slim, and he plays tennis.”

Rajiv laughed and said, “Looks like the case is solved.

CHAPTER 8

Arvind Chatterjee

30 m

A hero assigned to solve the murder of another hero. **@Bangalore Police** we thank you for assigning **@Rajiv Bakshi** to this case. I am sure Justice will be swift.

#bestofficerassigned #swiftjustice #bangalorepolicewelldone

589 Likes 88 Comments

As they re-entered the bedroom, Rajiv moved forward to closely investigating the lifeless body of Mr. Balaram. Evidently, he was stabbed in the stomach, multiple times, but the sharp object, probably a knife, was missing. The deceased was in his nightgown, and there were no other injury marks anywhere else. But something was not right about Mr. Balaram's expression. Normally, stabbing victims have a shocked and painful face, as it is their last expression. However, Mr. Balaram's expression was calm and composed.

"Did we find the murder weapon?"

"No, sir, we searched the room and the adjacent rooms but only found a cigarette bud in this room. Nothing else seems out of the way."

"Which brand?"

"Gold Flake Kings."

"Hari, is that the brand which Mr. Balaram used to smoke?"

"No, sir, Saab only smoked pipes, not cigarettes."

"Who smokes Gold Flake Kings in this house?"

"Vicky Saab."

"Did he used to smoke in front of Mr. Balaram?"

"No, sir, never."

"Ok. Mr. Dutta, please arrange to send the body for post mortem and arrange for the report ASAP."

"Sure, sir," Mr. Dutta replied and left the room.

Rajiv moved towards the antique chest in the room. "Did Mr. Balaram always use to keep large sum of money here, in the locker?"

"Yes, sir. Saabji felt proud about this locker and always kept it stacked."

"It does not have a keyhole! It is locked by a PIN?"

"Yes, sir."

"Does anyone know what the PIN is?"

"No, sir, no one in the house knows about it."

"Not even you?"

"Kya baat karte hein, sir? How will I know of the PIN, sir?"

"How much money does it have? Any estimate?"

"Not only money, sir; it has all legal documents too. I don't have much idea about the money it holds, but Saab once gave me five lakh rupees from it to deposit in a bank account."

"Which bank account? Do you know the name of it?"

"Yes, sir, it is an NGO for cancer treatment."

Rajiv turned to one of the police officers. "Mr. Goyal, please arrange for a locksmith to break this lock."

Mr. Goyal asked Rajiv, "Why, sir? I mean, any reasons? Do you suspect any theft? It is locked."

"The main door was also locked, and still we have a dead man here, and this is only a locker. Do as I say. Also, perform a fingerprint check of the locker."

"Ok, sir!" Mr. Goyal saluted affirmatively.

Rajiv moved towards the bookshelf now and explored the books. Most of them were legal books. Apart from them, only murder mysteries—around 30 crime dramas by renowned authors.

"Your Saab liked to read detective stories!"

"Yes, sir, he said that it gave him in depth knowledge of how a criminal's mind works. Also, he loved to read about how the criminals would set traps but eventually fall for justice. And then he would laugh and say, 'In the end, Justice must prevail'."

"Interesting character. Hope I would have met him sooner."

Rajiv moved towards the windows and explored them. He turned towards Hari and asked, "Are the windows always locked?"

"Only when it is cold or raining, like yesterday night."

Rajiv turned towards Mr. Dutta.

"Mr. Dutta, do you have anything else that you found suspicious?"

"Yes, sir, it drizzled yesterday night, so the lawn was wet. We have got footprints, just below this room, of someone coming towards the house and then going back."

"Wow! Just below this room, you say? Is it where the bathroom pipes lead down to?"

"Yes, sir."

"Interesting; send those foot prints for investigation."

"That is already done, sir."

"Ok, let's go and talk to the family members now."

"Whom do you want to start with?"

"Who lives just below this room?"

"That would be Mrs. Pubali, Mr. Balaram's only daughter."

"Let's start with her."

CHAPTER 9

India 4Life

@india4life

The Green Man serial killer case hero, @iamRajivBakshi has started the investigation of the murder of Former Chief Justice Balaram Shetty on a positive note. Room was locked from inside and the ventilator shaft in the washroom was open. Looks like someone who was sentenced by the deceased has taken his revenge. @BangalorePolice - whoever was sentenced by Chief Justice Balaram Shetty, take everyone in custody and get the truth out of them.

#ahugeloss #chiefjusticeneedsjustice #RIP #weneedjustice

11:58 AM · Feb 29, 2020 · Twitter Web App

793 Retweet **584** Comment **984** Likes

On his way out of the room, Rajiv called Mr. Dhole about the background check on all the siblings. As Mr. Dhole briefed him, Rajiv paused in his stride and listened in awe, like a baby listening to his mother's lullaby. All Rajiv responded during the whole conversation was with monosyllables like 'Hmm', 'Oh, is it?' and finally he said, "Are you sure about all of this?"

A proud Mr. Dhole beamed on the other side, having delivered a huge lead to the case.

Rajiv made his way to the ground floor and knocked on Mrs. Pubali Shetty's room. This room was just below Mr. Balaram's room. Mrs.

Pubali straightened up as she saw Rajiv walking in. "How can I help you, Inspector?"

"To start with, a glass of cold drinks would be fine."

Mrs. Pubali was surprised, but she hardly had any options than to get the drinks; so, she called for Hari. This gave Rajiv an opportunity to study the room. The structure was similar to that of Mr. Balaram's room. The bathroom and windows had the same edifice. The bed was not antique, rather a glitzy one. There were no showpieces or lockers and a large dressing table, which boasted of quite a few high-end cosmetics, replaced the mini library. Rajiv took this opportunity to take a good look at Mrs. Pubali too. She must be in her early 30s, but she maintained herself well enough. She had a square jaw, which complimented well with her round nose. Her beautiful face had just one flaw, a big mole on the left cheek, which would be the first thing anyone noticed in her face. She tried to hide it with concealers, but it was still visible. This jarred the otherwise pretty face. It made her look pissed off all the time, although she may have been in a jolly mood.

Rajiv opened with a lighter note, "How are you feeling, Mrs. Shetty?"

"Really scared, Inspector; how can anyone murder my father? That too, in our own home!"

"That too by one of your siblings or at least, someone from this house," Rajiv added emphatically.

"What do you mean, someone from the house? Do you think any of us did it? He was our father."

"I am not saying it, Mrs. Shetty, the evidence is."

"But what about the foot prints in the garden, the ventilator hole, or what if a thief did it?"

"We have sent the foot prints for analysis, and thieves don't kill. However, the ventilator hole indeed is interesting. By the way, the pipe beside the ventilator hole, it lands right beside your window. Did you see anyone coming towards the house or hear anything? If there was a thief or somebody from outside, you must have heard him going up the pipe by your window or coming down the pipe!"

Pubali was sweating but kept a straight face and responded, "No, yesterday night was cold, and it was drizzling too, so I kept the window closed and fell asleep. I did not hear anything."

"Nothing! Your room is just below Mr. Balaram's room. You must have heard something, like someone going up the stairs, someone coming down, someone knocking the door, any footsteps, any chaos, anything! Your father got murdered, so there must have been a lot of commotion. Are you sure you heard nothing?"

"Actually, I have insomnia. I take sleeping pills every night, which helps me with a sound sleep."

"Can I have a look at the sleeping pills, please?"

Pubali was surprised by this odd request, but she complied.

"So, what happened yesterday? Can you tell me everything that involved Mr. Balaram?"

"Nothing much. When I came back home in the evening, Dad already had his dinner. Therefore, I could not meet him. I just went to my room and read a book. Around midnight, I took my sleeping pill and fell asleep."

"When did you fall asleep? Any idea?"

"Must be around half past midnight."

"And you did not hear anything suspicious or joyful?"

"Joyful! Why would I hear something cheerful past midnight?"

Rajiv added a sarcastic pinch in his tone now, "Aah! Looks like you do not know of it. So, it's not only me who forgets his close one's birthday."

Pubali sulked but her defiant instinct took over. "Unlike you, I did not forget about Dad's birthday. However, we don't celebrate Dad's birthday at midnight. He is an old man, and you have to respect his age. He needs rest. We had plans to celebrate today, but unfortunately..."

Rajiv replied, "It is evident that you love your father very much, and I am sorry for your loss. Do you suspect anybody? What about your siblings? Do you suspect anyone of them?"

Pubali irritably turned her face towards Rajiv and with disgust, she said, "None of my brothers can do this; all of us loved our father a lot."

"Ok, then anybody outside the family who might have done this?"

"No, Inspector, I cannot think of anyone who hated my father so much as to take his life."

"I acknowledge that and appreciate it too, Mrs. Shetty; however, someone must have stabbed your father. There are clear stab wounds, which led to his death. If you cannot think of anyone outside your family, who could have done this, then, I have fewer options than to focus my investigation to members of this house only."

Pubali, being cornered, looked around for a way to divert attention from herself and her brothers. After a brief thought, she responded, "Now that you stress on it, there is indeed a possibility. It must be sixteen or seventeen years ago, when Dad gave a jail sentence to a goon for possession of illegal weapons. If I remember correctly, his name was Vikas Kumar. I recall that a few days before Dad could give his final judgment, Vikas Kumar's goons attacked Dad's car when he was on his way to work. Dad and our family were given police protection after that incident, until Vikas Kumar was sentenced to jail. After his sentence, Vikas Kumar had openly threatened Dad that he would kill him and our family. I am not sure if that is related to this case; however, that is the only person whom I can think of at the moment."

"Is it? I was not aware of it, and I shall look into it."

Rajiv paused for few seconds to inspect the sleeping pills and then resumed "I am led to believe that you are married. I can't see your husband anywhere; is he around?"

Now, Rajiv had crossed the line in to her private life. Bad move. "Inspector, I am sorry to say this, but either you are a dumb police officer who rose in rank only because you are old, or you are smart enough to do a background check on me before coming here, and you very well know, that I am fighting a divorce case with my husband. In that case, you intently wanted to hurt the sentiments of a noble tax-paying citizen by asking that question. Which one is it—are you dumb or are you shrewd?"

"Mrs. Shetty, I am old, and that age has given me the experience to believe that you are not telling me everything about yesterday night. You are hiding something from me, and I assure you that I am shrewd enough to find out what you are hiding. If I can find it out, you will know the answer to your question. Till then, think of a better story than an insomniac having a sound sleep."

Rajiv dashed out of the room.

CHAPTER 10

ArpitaTalukdar

♡ ◯ ▽ ⊓

1346 likes

ArpitaTalukdar Killing someone is of course a sin but killing someone on his or her birthday is evil.

#murderermustbepunished #JusticeforBalaramShetty #swiftactionneeded

View all 159 comments

58 MINUTES AGO

Rajiv was about to make his way to the youngest son's room at the ground floor, but traced back his steps and decided against it and went upstairs. Once up the stairs, he turned right and knocked on Vicky Shetty's room. Vicky looked distraught and welcomed Rajiv half-heartedly.

"Hi, Mr. Vicky, I am Rajiv Bakshi, and I am in charge of the case about your father's murder. Do you mind if we discuss for a few minutes his sad demise?"

"No, Inspector, not at all. I would be happy to help, but there is not much that I know."

"You are the eldest son of Mr. Balaram?"

"Yes, Inspector."

Rajiv took a pause to look around. The room was a mess, like any other bachelor's room. The room was spacious and airy and had two big windows. It had two other doors inside, one opening up to a balcony and the other leading to the rest room. There were no centerpieces or other attractions to the blunt room, only a study table and two chairs. Mr. Vicky looked to be in his late 30s and had an average height. A tummy stood out from an otherwise lanky figure, portraying his addiction to alcohol. He donned a pair of hard-rimmed specs, which did not do much to hide his age, and he sported an anchor style beard around the chin and a moustache. He had short, receding hair, which had already commenced its journey to eventual baldness.

“You are supposed to be the most mature among your brothers and sisters; so, I am going to come to the point straight away, if you don't mind.”

“Not at all.”

“When was the last time you met your father?”

“Yesterday, in the morning. I had a short conversation with him in the breakfast table before leaving for work.”

“And where do you work?”

“I am a chemical engineer at a private firm.”

“Interesting; so, what was your last discussion with your father about?”

“Casual. It was like, 'hi, hello', you know, 'how are you doing Dad' kind.”

“Today is your father's birthday; didn't you wish him at midnight? Didn't you discuss anything about his birthday plans?”

“No, Inspector, I am not good with dates, and I did not remember till today morning.”

“But your sister, Mrs. Shetty, said that yesterday, all of you were planning for a party today!"

Vicky was caught off guard but without even blinking, he said, "They must have been planning with my other brothers. I was in work for the whole day and returned late; so, they might have missed informing me. I got to know of it today morning only."

"I have been told that you went for a morning walk today morning. Do you go for morning walk every day? Or, today was something special?"

"No, I am not a regular jogger, but I could not sleep well last night. Actually, I could not sleep at all, and recently, my health has not been well. Therefore, I thought I would start jogging and make it a habit. As they say, it's never too late to start, and indeed, today was the first day."

"I am afraid you picked a wrong day to start doing the right thing. As you are the only one who left Kunj Villa after your father was murdered, I may have to ask you a few questions, which may sound baseless to you, but are important for me. Where did you go for jogging?"

"Not a problem Inspector, I can understand, and I am willing to co-operate. I went to a park near the house to jog. After that, I went to a nearby lake, sat there for a while, and returned home."

"Did you go to any store, tea stall or anywhere else? Did you meet with someone who can verify your story?"

"No, Inspector, as I said, today was my first day, so I do not have any friends in the jogging park yet. I didn't go to any store either, and I planned to have my morning tea at home, so, negative on the tea stall too."

Rajiv took a momentary pause and whispered to himself, "And still they tell me, why do you suspect everyone?"

Rajiv resumed, "Ok, let's keep that point aside for now. You mentioned that you didn't sleep well yesterday night, and your room is close to Mr. Balaram's room, so you must have heard something yesterday night!"

"Umm, well, no. I don't think so."

"Are you sure, Mr. Vicky? A man was murdered in the next room, someone climbed the pipes and got in and out of the house, and still you did not hear anything? I am sure you understand that it sounds quite suspicious."

Vicky attempted to put stress to his memories. "Now that I think of it, I heard someone going up the stairs around 2 am."

"Okay, anything more? Come on, Mr. Vicky, you did not sleep for the whole night; you must have heard something else too."

"I may have heard someone at the corridor or at Dad's room at around 3 am. I am not exactly sure where it was coming from."

"Are you sure of the time?"

"I am sure that I heard something at 2 am as I went to the balcony for a smoke at 5 minutes past two. The one I heard at 3 am is dicey. I am assuming it was an hour after I went for the smoke."

"Did it not arouse any suspicion? Didn't you go to check on your father? All the rooms in this house have an attached bath, so why would anyone roam about in the night?"

"Dad calls Hari sometimes at the middle of the night by buzzing the bell. I must have thought that it was Hari."

"But you would hear the bell ring in that case, wouldn't you?"

Vicky looked a frustrated figure now. "I understand how it sounds, Inspector, but I did not even pay attention to those sounds. I didn't try to find the reason for it at that point of time, but I surely wish now, that I would go out of my room to check it out. I could never have imagined that someone would murder my Dad, so those suspicions never got aroused."

"Talking about suspicions, who from the family do you think did this?"

Vicky turned red. "I think you are not thinking straight! No one from our family would do this! All of us loved him very much and respected him. It must be an outsider. I am sure the person whose footprints were found in the lawn murdered Dad. Dad has given many harsh sentences to criminals during his days as a High Court judge. One of them must have taken his revenge by killing him. You need to find the killer, Inspector."

"Rest assured, the killer will be found, but let's suppose we assume that someone from Kunj Villa killed him. Who would be your primary suspect?"

"No, Inspector, none of my brothers can do that."

"When did I say it has to be your brothers? You are not much of a fan of women power, I see. It's trending on the internet Mr. Vicky. Also, we cannot forget about Hari."

"No, Inspector, none of them can do it, never. Hari has been with us since childhood; he is a part of the family, and no one among us would even think of killing my Dad."

"Hmm, ok, let's recap. So, you did not go to your Dad's room yesterday?"

"No, not at all."

"You know Mr. Vicky, it's not a crime to go to your Dad's room. You can tell me if you have."

"What do you mean? Why would I lie about it? I don't have anything to hide!"

Rajiv lit a cigarette and said, "A cigarette butt has been found from your father's room, of the same brand that you smoke. Hari had cleaned the room yesterday evening. So, unless you went to your father's room after yesterday evening, I do not see how that butt can be in that room."

Rajiv's composure was strongly opposed by a vehement reaction from Vicky. "What do you mean, Inspector? Am I the only one who smokes this brand in Bangalore? It can be your officers too, and I do not smoke in front of Dad, so there is no chance of that."

"Why, were you afraid of your father?"

"I don't know what family you come from, Inspector, but it is not respectful to smoke in front of your father in our family."

"Yes, but a dead body cannot see you smoke, so, technically, there is no disrespect in smoking in front of your father's corpse."

"Inspector, you are crossing your limits! Are you trying to imply that I murdered my father and then smoked a cigarette in his room, beside his dead body? Do you know how disturbing it sounds?"

"That butt has been sent for a fingerprint scan. If your finger prints are found, this disturbing explanation would be the only explanation, because, in your family, you do not smoke in front of your father, at least till he is alive."

"That's it. I do not want to talk to you anymore Inspector. You may leave, and next time, you will need to talk to my lawyer to speak to me because you do not have the manners to speak to a respected citizen of the country."

"If your finger print is found in the butt, it would take a great lawyer to stop me from arresting you. So, get a good one."

CHAPTER 11

Arvind Chatterjee

46 m

@Bangalore Police &@Rajiv Bakshi wasting time in interrogating family members whereas the outsider who came in, murdered, and left through the vent roams free. By now, the murderer must have left Bangalore. Don't they get it? The door was locked from the inside; no one inside the house can have anything to do with it. Even I can do a better job than this lazy shit.

#weneedabetterpoliceforce #uselesspolice #lazyRajiv

#murdererroamsfree

3k Likes 789 Comments

Rajiv left Mr. Vicky's room defiantly. He looked happy with himself. A pissed off interviewee is a triumphant interview in Rajiv's profession. He took a left turn from Mr. Balaram's room and knocked on Ronit's room.

"Hi, Mr. Ronit, my name is Rajiv Bakshi, and I am investigating your father's death. May I come in?"

A five-feet-five-inch mid-thirties man stood up and welcomed Rajiv inside the room. Unlike his elder brother, Mr. Ronit looked quite a stud with his extended goatee style beard and a fit physique. He did not have a muscular body, but he must have had a good metabolism, which kept him hale and hearty. The room looked like it was recently cleaned, maybe today. It did not have any balconies, but like all other rooms of Kunj Villa, had an en suite bathroom. Apart from the regulars, it had two big wardrobes, and the walls were covered with *Harry Potter*, *Game of Thrones*, and *Breaking Bad* posters. In a corner of the room was an X-Box connected to a 40-inch TV. However, on the left wall, there was a showpiece of a shield with two swords, cross-tangled, which was a complete contrast to everything else in the room.

Ronit welcomed Rajiv. "Yes sure, please Inspector. Did you find anything? Did Dad kill himself? Why would he do that? It makes no sense."

"Kill himself? I can assure you Mr. Ronit that the case isn't that simple. He was murdered. You can be surprised, but, most probably, someone from this family committed this heinous crime."

"What! You can't be serious about that! He was our father. Why would any of us do that? And the door was locked from within. I am sure the murderer was someone whom Dad had sentenced previously. He is out of jail now and taking his revenge. He must have come via the toilet duct. Didn't you see the boot marks in the garden?"

"Seconds ago, you were confident that your father committed suicide, and now you are certain that he was murdered by an outsider?"

Ronit composed himself and said, "I am just listing down the possibilities."

"Mr. Ronit, going through the possibilities and filtering the facts out is our job, and we are very good at it too. Please do not stress your brain on those things. I need you to use your brains on other pressing matters. Can you please tell me about yesterday? Did you meet your father in the morning, at breakfast?"

"No, I had left for work quite early and did not see him for the whole day."

"Not even at night?"

"No, I returned around 8 pm at night, asked Hari to bring my dinner to my room, and then went to sleep at midnight."

"So, you did not see your father even once yesterday?"

"No and that's my biggest regret."

"Where do you work?"

"In a small IT firm."

"Did you hear anything yesterday night? From your father's room?"

"No, not much."

"Mr. Ronit, I need you to lay stress on your memory. Did you hear any kind of sounds, footsteps, voices, or any other sound yesterday night? Your room is close to Mr. Balaram's room, you must have heard something! As you said, a burglar broke in and killed your father and still you didn't hear anything! You must have heard something."

Ronit thought for a second and said, "I do not remember clearly, but I think I heard a female voice from Dad's room. I cannot be sure of it, though."

"At what time was it?"

"I cannot be sure. I am not even sure if I heard the voice."

"Ok, that's still helpful. Do you leave alone?"

Mr. Ronit was caught off guard with the sudden change of the subject. He mumbled, "Yes, my wife committed suicide about 6 months ago."

"What! Why would that be?"

"I myself think about the same question all the time. The only probable answer might be that I wasn't a good husband, that's why."

"As in, you used to physically abuse her or did you cheat on her?"

“I would not have said this to you, but the gravity of the present matter deserves complete honesty from my end. I was having an affair with an office colleague. My wife caught us in a vulnerable moment, and she suffered from depression since then.”

“When and where did she catch you?”

“About one year before her death, in a hotel room.”

“And how did she come to know of your affair?”

“My Dad was a suspicious man. He could read everyone's mind from his or her behavior. My Dad adored Sabitri, my wife. We had been married for 4 years when my affair with Rumela started. Everything went fine for almost a year, but, I don't know how, my Dad got suspicious about me. He hired a detective, Akash Bose, to check on me.”

Rajiv stopped him there. He was astounded, “Akash Bose, the detective who was involved in the Green Man serial killer case?”

Ronit nodded affirmatively. Rajiv chuckled and said, “That octopus has his tentacles everywhere. Yes, please carry on.”

“One day, Dad called me to his room. He showed me some intimate pictures of Rumela and myself and slammed me for cheating on my wife. He ordered me to stop my affair. He threatened me that if I did not stop my affair, he would inform Sabitri about it. Can you believe it? My own father was blackmailing me.”

“He was doing it for your own good.”

“Yeah, I know, but at that moment, the fact that I was being blackmailed by my father did not sit with me correctly. I became rebellious. If anyone else had blackmailed me, I would have stopped my affair, but my own father! I defied him and ignored his threats. Till date, I regret that decision. If only I had stopped my affair, I would not have lost so many things in life.”

“What happened then?”

"When Detective Akash Bose confirmed to my father that I had not stopped the affair, my father was devastated. He tried multiple times to talk me out of it, but I was enraged at him and did not take his threats or advice seriously. Finally, my father ruined my life; he informed Sabitri about my affair, as he had threatened. Since that day, all peace and pleasure in my life has disappeared. Every single day, I had to put up with Sabitri's sentimental drama and her deplorable cries. I stopped my affair, but still, she could not come out of depression, rather, she sunk more into it. The whole family tried to help her, but she loved me too much. One day, I came back from office and found her lying lifeless in her bed, her wrists bleeding and a blood-bathed knife on the floor. Till now, that image haunts me, every single day."

"Was there a police investigation?"

"Yes there was; the investigation went on for more than 2 weeks, if I remember correctly."

"Ok, fine, Mr. Ronit. I truly feel sad for your misfortunes and I hope, in the coming days, I need to trouble you as less as possible. You mentioned about your father having adversaries outside of this family, due to his profession. Can you think of anyone in particular who could have murdered your father yesterday night?"

Ronit spared few seconds to think about it and said, "There was one called Vikas Kumar; he had threatened Dad and our family."

"Yes, Mrs. Shetty told us about him. You said there are many; so, anyone else that you can think of?"

Ronit took a few seconds to recollect and resumed, "Around 15 years back, Dad mediated a case about a lady who killed her husband as he wanted to sell their 10-year-old daughter to pimps. I do not remember her name, but the police arrested her and presented her case to Dad. It was an open-and-shut case. She had confessed that she committed the murder. However, she begged my father, not to punish her, as there will be no one to look after her daughter. Dad did not want to, but the law tied his hands.

He gave a 14-year sentence to that woman and advised her daughter to be moved to a care home. 4 years later, her daughter committed suicide as she was repeatedly raped in the care home. When Dad heard about this, he was heartbroken. He blamed himself for the tortures that the daughter had to go through. He even went to visit the woman in jail, to apologize to her, but that woman was enraged at the news of her daughter's suicide. As soon as she saw Dad, she ran towards him with rage, strangled Dad, and choked him. She tried to kill him. Thankfully, police officers were nearby. They intruded and pulled the woman out of the tussle. The woman threatened aloud that whenever she came out of prison, she would kill our Dad, as she believed he was responsible for her daughter's death and torture. She screamed that she knew care homes are hotspots for prostitution; hence, she had requested Dad to let her go. Frankly speaking, I think Dad knew this may happen, but he had no other options than to give the jail sentence. Law bound him. My Dad always repented that judgment and often sobbed about it to us.

Rajiv listened eagerly, thanked Ronit for his time, and left the room.

Rajiv made his way downstairs where Mr. Dhole was already waiting for him. Rajiv went up to him and said, "Crazy family, everyone's got a story; did you send the body for post mortem?"

"Yes, sir, the report would be with us by the next three days."

"Ok, I am leaving for the day; we will meet at 9 am tomorrow."

"Sir, are you done interviewing everyone?"

"No, not the eldest son."

"Do you want me to do that?"

"They have got a young child, Mr. Dhole. I don't want that child to have a rash memory of a police officer interviewing him or their parents. I will come in normal clothes tomorrow, and then we can talk to that family, not before that."

"Ok, sir, noted."

"You please ask your team to keep a close watch on everyone. None of them are trustworthy."

"Why, sir, do you have doubts on anyone?"

"No, not anyone, everyone. All of them are hiding something; I can sense it."

Mr. Dhole exclaimed, "If they are hiding something, I can use my methods to get it out of them. Shall I?"

"Not necessary. We only need to pull one loose thread, and the whole family will crumble automatically. I think this is a disconnected and selfish family. Mr. Balaram was the only thread holding it together, and sadly, with his demise, this bunch of fools just need a nudge, and all of them will start slinging mud at each other. We just need to make that nudge."

"I did not understand, sir."

"No worries, I will give a demonstration soon, and then it would be easier for you. Meanwhile, you please look at the death of Mrs. Sabitri, wife of Mr. Ronit. We might get some clues from there. Please brief me by tomorrow morning on it."

"Anything else Sir?"

"Yes, look at the records of all the jail terms that Mr. Balaram Shetty had sentenced during his days as a High Court Judge and check which of them were released from jail over the last 2 years. Also, please get me details about Vikas Kumar, as he was also sentenced by Mr. Balaram. Finally, please look at the records of a woman whom Mr. Balaram had sentenced about 15 years ago for murdering her husband. He had a daughter who committed suicide in a care home."

"Ok, sir, you will get the report by tomorrow morning."

CHAPTER 12

Daring Darling

@daredal

36 hours passed by. Someone who served justice to criminals in our country is still crying for his own justice. I cry with you too, sir, and I will fight for you, to get you the justice you deserve. The @BangalorePolice has found nothing concrete yet, nor arrested anyone. If we stay quiet, they will soon declare this a suicide and wash their hands off it. We can't stay quite. We have to fight.

#IstandforBalaramShetty #catchthemurderer #fightwithme

#netizensmustrise

10:12 AM · Mar 1, 2020 ·Twitter Web App

912 Retweet **546** Comment **4327** Likes

Sporting a bright ping skirt, Rajiv knocked on the doors of the ground floor room of Kuntal and Aparajita. As he was welcomed inside, Rajiv noticed the drastic differences of the other brother's room to this one. It had three large wardrobes, which took up most of the space in the room. There were few pictures of the couple, but predominantly, the walls were filled with pictures of Sparsh since his childhood days. A picture of Kuntal's in-laws was also there but no picture of the full Shetty family.

Evidently, Sparsh was a naughty kid, as the whole room looked a mess, toys ruled over the floor and sofa. Aparajita quickly apologized, but Rajiv explained that he has a daughter too and her bedroom is always a mess. Rajiv took a quick look at Aparajita. She must have been married in her teens or early 20s, going by Sparsh's age. She was pretty but feisty. It was evident from her assertiveness that she was a no nonsense woman and a strict mother. A decent height of 5ft 6 inches enriched the aura of her appearance, but her face had a pinch of tiredness to it, the result of parenting. If she had the cosmetics collection that Mrs. Pubali had, she would definitely be catching quite a few eyes of the neighbors, but she hardly got time for herself.

Kuntal soon joined them and immediately put forward a request. "Inspector, we know you want to talk to us, but can we do it outside of the room please? We do not want Sparsh to hear about it."

Rajiv looked up to Kuntal's innocent looking face. He must have got married at an early age too, as he would hardly be 30 now, and he already had a 7-year-old kid. Rajiv assumed that it must have been a love marriage as they got married at such an early age, whereas the eldest son of the family has not married yet. Kuntal was clean shaven and wore a pair of rim less eyeglasses. His cheeks were puffy but he had a stout figure. He was about 6 feet tall but had a poor dressing sense. He was wearing a rugged trouser with a shirt. It made him look older than Rajiv himself. The standout feature about Kuntal was a beautiful smile in his face, which prolonged forever.

Rajiv answered, "But I am here to talk to Sparsh only. I will talk to him first and then I shall have a word with both of you."

"But Inspector, he does not know about his granddad's death. He would be devastated if he comes to know about it."

Rajiv reassured to Kuntal, "Don't' worry, I will not talk to him about the sad demise of your father. I am a father too, and I can understand your concern. As you can see, I came in plainclothes today, as I do not want that young soul to think that he is talking to a police officer. You need to introduce me to him as a friend of yours."

Aparajita requested, "But, Inspector, is it absolutely necessary? He does not know anything."

"Yes, Madam, it is absolutely necessary that I talk to him. Please tell him that I am a friend of Mr. Kuntal, and then, I can take over from there."

Aparajita loathed the idea but hardly had any other choice. She went inside to call Sparsh. Meanwhile Rajiv quickly asked, "What have you told them about the police in the house?"

Kuntal quickly responded, "Police is nothing new to Sparsh. About a year ago, when Sabitri Bhabhi was killed, the police stormed the house, kept coming for days, and interrogated everyone, just like now. The police officer in charge was not as considerate as you, and he interrogated Sparsh for 30 minutes, while in police uniform. Can you imagine? 30 minutes! Sparsh was shaking when he came out. Since then, whenever police used to come to our house, we told him they have come to find 'Sona Maa', that's what he used to call Sabitri Bhabhi. We told him that Sabitri Bhabhi was playing hide and seek and police are trying to find her in the house. Sparsh adored his Sona Maa; she was like a second mother to him. When she left us, Sparsh used to wait the whole day for her to return, and every night, he would cry himself to sleep. He has already gone through a lot, so I would request you to re-consider talking to him."

"I understand your concerns and sincerely apologize on behalf of the police force, for this improper behavior by the previous investigation officer. I will find out who he was, and I assure you he will come and apologize to you for what he has done. If you deem necessary, he will also apologize to Sparsh. However, for now, I really need to talk to Sparsh, alone. I would never say anything to him to hurt him. I am a father too, and I would never speak roughly to a young mind. It imprints that rough behavior and latches on to their small basket of memories. I know that, so please relax and kindly introduce him to myself and please excuse yourself from the room."

First look at Sparsh, and it made Rajiv's day. He was like a cute little angel, his cheeks were tomato red, and he had a fair complexion. He had curly hair, like Maggi, which made him look adorable. As Kuntal introduced Rajiv to Sparsh, the cute little angel wished him good morning. Rajiv forgot he was on duty, kneeled down, and hugged Sparsh. Kuntal and Aparajita were much relaxed now. They excused themselves from the room, pretending to step away to get some breakfast for Rajiv.

Rajiv was just thinking about how to make Sparsh comfortable and how he could make Sparsh trust him, but it did not take any of his planning to work the charm. Sparsh was a smart, curious, and talkative boy. He started to question Rajiv on everything about Rajiv's life, and Rajiv had no answers for most of them and mostly reacted with a laugh or a facial expression, silently and surprisingly expressing, "I don't know!" Sparsh kept on bombarding him with questions.

"How do you know my Daddy?" "What is your favorite toy?" "Do you have a baby?" "How old is he?" "Why didn't you bring him here to play with me?" "Does your mother scold you too?" "My mother does not let me play and always asks me to study." "Do you know about Avengers?" "Which character do you want to be?" And the questions continued till Rajiv had to put a full stop to it.

"Are you going to question me only? Or will I get a chance to question you too?"

Finally, Rajiv got silence in return, a chance to play his hand. "Who is your favorite Marvel's character?"

"I want to be Black Panther."

"Black Panther! Why so?"

"Because he is a King and a superhero."

"Wow! I must say it's a smart choice. Next question, what do you love more, ice cream or Chocolate?"

This is every child's dilemma, to choose between two of their favorite desserts. Sparsh took some time to answer and finally settled for ice cream.

Rajiv continued, “Ok, now a tough one; do you want to be a detective or a police officer?”

Sparsh spontaneously responded, “Detective, I want to be a detective.”

“Do you love detective stories? Does your granddad tell you those stories? I saw many detective books in his room.”

“Yes, 'Dadu' is my partner. He is Dr. Watson, and I am Sherlock Holmes.”

“Is it? You are Sherlock Holmes? Are you sure? Then I will have to verify it, because Sherlock Holmes is supposed to be smart,and he knows many secrets.”

“I am smart, and I know secrets too.”

“Oh, do you? Ok, let's see. How can we test if you are Sherlock Holmes.” Rajiv pretended to think, took his time, and then said, “Do you go to your granddad's room often?”

“Yes, I always play with Dadu in his room.”

“Did you see a locker in his room?”

“Yes, I play with that too.”

“You need to know a 6 digit number to open that lock. Let me see how smart you are. Can you tell me that 6 digit code?”

Sparsh excitedly stood up in his sofa. “Password for that safe! I do not know the password, but I asked Dadu to tell me the password and he told me that our family is the password.”

“Why did you ask Dadu for the password? You are supposed to find it yourself, as you are Sherlock Holmes.”

Sparsh responded, “I didn't want to ask Dadu, but the day before yesterday, Dad insisted that I ask Dadu about it, and he told me that it is our secret. So, I asked Dadu but did not tell him that Dad requested me to ask him this question. After all, it was mine and my Dad's secret."

"Well done Sparsh; that was very good. Let me see if I have any gifts for you in my pocket." Rajiv brought out a Dairy Milk Cadbury from his pocket and gifted to Sparsh. Sparsh became ecstatic.

Rajiv asked, "Should I ask a final question to finalize, if you are Sherlock Holmes or Dr. Watson?"

Sparsh was busy opening the Dairy Milk chocolate and did not respond. May be he did not even hear the question correctly. Rajiv tapped Sparsh for his attention, but the Dairy Milk in Sparsh's right hand gripped all of it. Rajiv took out another Dairy Milk and swayed in front of Sparsh. Now he had his attention.

"I will ask you one final question to check if you are Sherlock Holmes or Dr. Watson."

Sparsh happily nodded his head.

"Do you know Sparsh, that, Sherlock Holmes could sense everything, even when he was sleeping?"

"Yes, Dadu told me about his super powers."

"So, can you tell me, yesterday night, when you were sleeping, did your Mom or Dad leave your side? Let's see now if you are Sherlock Holmes."

"Yes I am Sherlock Holmes. Mom and Dad both left my side twice. First time was soon after I went to sleep. Actually I was pretending to sleep. Second, Dad only left my side during the night, but Mom was there by my side. Dad came back after sometime."

"So, Mr. Sherlock Holmes, I present to you this chocolate. You are indeed very bright."

Sparsh smiled and punched in the air, with joy.

Rajiv said "So, what about your favorite color?"

Sparsh said "I love blue; I even have a blue pencil box."

"Wow, and what about your favorite cartoon character?" Rajiv kept on chipping few favorite questions so that Sparsh did not understand what damage he had done for his parents, kissed him in the forehead, waved goodbye, and left the room.

As soon as Rajiv came outside, Aparajita and Kuntal sprinted inside the room. Their pounding heart finally found some succor when they saw Sparsh happily eating the Dairy Milk. Rajiv signaled the couple to meet him in the kitchen urgently.

CHAPTER 13

India 4Life

@india4life

I agree with @daredal, we need to raise our voice for late Mr. Balaram Shetty. There is no positive news coming out of the investigation and time is slipping by. @iamRajivBakshi is not taking any positive actions. Looks like his age has caught up with him. @BangalorePolice pass the case to a more compatible and young officer who can act fast. If we continue at this pace, we would not be able to catch the killer by the next leap year even.

#replaceRajivBakshi #chiefjusticeneedsjustice

#slowpoliceworksucks #weneedjustice

4:44 PM · Mar 1, 2020 ·Twitter Web App

1036 Retweet **2563** Comment **9836** Likes

Aparajita praised Rajiv for his kind behavior with Sparsh, a stark opposite to their previous encounter with Indian Police. Rajiv responded with a question, "About Mrs. Sabitri's death? Was it a suicide or do you suspect any foul play?"

Aparajita responded, "Of course it was a suicide. Bhabhi was very depressed during those days. We should have been more careful with her and should not have left her alone in her room. We could have prevented it. If only, we consulted a psychiatrist, she would be here with us."

"And why was she depressed?" Rajiv was testing the sibling bond now.

Kuntal whispered, "We should not be saying this, but Ronit Bhaiya had an affair with an office colleague, and Dad leaked it to Sabitri Bhabhi."

Rajiv acted surprised. "Mr. Ronit must have been very angry with Mr. Balaram!"

Now, Aparajita whispered, "Yes, he even threatened to kill my father-in-law."

"Are you sure he threatened to kill him?"

"Yes, of course, he threatened him in front of all of us."

"Ok, then we have a strong suspect."

Kuntal's bond of blood kicked in, "No, Inspector, nothing like that. Ronit Bhaiya threatened out of rage and under influence of alcohol. He would never do that. He loves Dad."

"Mr. Kuntal, no one threatens someone in peace. Usually, people threaten when they are on the tipping point of rage. Please do not try to defend your brother. However, can you tell me about the day Mr. Balaram died? When did you last meet Mr. Balaram?"

As per Indian penal code, lying to a police officer is a criminal offence. Aparajita just became a criminal offender. "On the day before yesterday, we saw my father-in-law in the morning only. We had breakfast together."

"Was anyone else in that table, during breakfast?"

"No, it was just us."

"Are you sure, Mrs. Aparajita?"

"Yes Inspector, why wouldn't I be?"

"My. Vicky told us that he was having breakfast with Mr. Balaram, so he should have been on that table too."

Aparajita fumbled but quickly used Sparsh as her shield. "May be, we had left the table early, as Sparsh had to be ready for school. May be he came after we left."

Rajiv nodded suspiciously and said, "Ok. So, what did Mr. Balaram say during breakfast?"

"The usual; he asked about Sparsh's school and Kuntal's work."

"It was his birthday yesterday. Didn't you or Mr. Kuntal or Sparsh wish him at midnight?"

Kuntal told half-truths, "No, we did not wish him at midnight, as we were planning to throw a surprise party yesterday, but unfortunately, it was too late. Dad didn't like to be disturbed at night, so we never used to wish him at night."

"If I were to tell you someone from this house murdered your Dad, who would be your prime suspect?"

Aparajita and Kuntal both exclaimed, "What! No! No one from this house would do that. Never. All of us loved Dad and respected him. We are all his son and daughter; we can't murder him!"

"Then how do you think he was killed?"

"The footprints outside the house, someone must have come in through the ventilator in the toilet and murdered him. Dad's room's door was also locked from the inside. No one inside the house could have got in and come out of the room."

"What if someone inside the house locked the doors of Mr. Balaram's room from inside and then made his way out through the shaft?"

Aparajita leaped into self-defense, "But the foot marks are bi-directional, they come from the main gate towards Kunj Villa and then, back towards the main gate. So, someone must have come from outside."

"Fair point, we shall investigate on that front too. Has Mr. Balaram left any will which documents the division of his properties?"

Kuntal choked for a moment but Aparajita denied awareness of any will and said, "Presently we are not thinking about it, but it should be divided equally."

"You know, I also have a daughter, a few years older than Sparsh. When she was about Sparsh's age, I could hardly sleep any night. She used to disturb us so much. Is Sparsh the same? Or does he let you two sleep?"

No parents would let go of the chance to complain about insomnia after having a child. Aparajita and Kuntal were no different; they opened their heart out about insomnia, since Sparsh came into to their life.

Now that the couple confessed of insomnia, Rajiv laid his next question, "So, as you two were largely awake for the whole night, did you hear any kind of sounds yesterday night? A murderer came in and murdered your father. There must have been some sounds which both of you would have heard. Can you please stress your mind and think if you heard any kind of sounds on the night that Mr. Balaram was murdered?"

Aparajita said, "Yes, I think I heard footsteps, upstairs, multiple times, and even I heard someone going up the stairs around 2 am." Kuntal also vouched for the same.

"Ok, thanks for that. About the locker in your Dad's room, do you have any idea how much cash it may hold!"

The couple was taken aback at the sudden shift of topic. "No, we don't have any idea, but if I have to take a guess, I would say 8 to 10 lakhs. Dad liked to keep some cash with him, always."

"That's a lot of money to keep in your home, don't you think?"

"Yes, we told Dad multiple times to deposit it in bank and use an ATM card but he was not tech savvy and liked things to stay old school. So, he brought the locker."

"Do you know what would be the password for that locker?"

Kuntal vehemently denied, "No, how can we know? No one in the house other than my father knew about it. He never disclosed it to anyone."

With a cunning smile, Rajiv enquired, "Not even to Sparsh?"

Kuntal and Aparajita were sweating now but still did not let their guard down. "Sparsh would be the last person that my Dad would tell about it. He was strict about monetary affairs and did not like if anyone poked their nose in his financials. So, none of us, least of all, Sparsh, ever enquired about any such thing to my Dad."

"Did you ever try to guess or know, what can be the code? I mean it's so intriguing. Like a secret, waiting to be unfolded, that too in your own house. This must have crossed your mind to know about the code of the locker!"

"Never; it never crossed our mind."

Suddenly, Rajiv stood up from his chair, and in an instant, his smiling face turned into a frown and the mild voice geared up to the zone of a shout, "Then why did you ask Sparsh to find out the code?"

Kuntal and Aparajita were surprised at this sudden vocal attack, and a shiver went down their spines. They sulked and could not find any place to hide their face, as they had been caught blatantly lying. They initially resorted to silence but when Rajiv shouted at them again, Kuntal shouted back, "Because I need money. I need money to pay for a flat that I have booked. We want to move out from here. We thought if we knew how much money there was in the locker, we could ask Dad accordingly."

"Why do you want to move out, and why did you lie?"

"I thought you won't understand or believe our cause. We thought that you would think that we wanted to steal it."

"Yes you are right, I do believe you wanted to steal it, but that is secondary as of now. Why do you want to move out?"

"Because this room is too small for 3 members in our family, and Sparsh is growing up; he needs his own room. We thought we would ask the money from Dad. He would surely understand how tough it is for the three of us to stay in a single room. The room is big, but still, it's a single room."

"You should not have lied to me. Tell me, are you hiding anything more from me? I am giving you a chance to come clean; otherwise, if I find it out later on, it will not be good for both of you."

Kuntal bravely said, "No Inspector, we are not hiding anything."

Rajiv had them cornered and now to hunt them down, he needed to confidently lie. He had a hunch, but the only way to be sure about it is to make the couple confess about it. "Ok, then tell me, Mr. Kuntal. The night Mr. Balaram died, what were you doing in Mr. Balaram's room at 3 am in the night?"

Kuntal was shivering but still stood his ground. "What are you saying, Inspector? I did not go to Dad's room that night; why would I go to his room?"

"You need to answer that to me, and not the other way round. Tell me, why did you go to your Dad's room? Mr. Vicky saw you going inside your Dad's room at 3 am in the night. Why are you lying to me? What are you hiding? What were you doing in his room? Tell me the truth or else I will arrest you right now."

Kuntal was fumbling. "Vicky Bhaiya saw me?"

"Yes he did, he heard your footsteps in the stairs, peeped through his keyhole, and saw you going inside Mr. Balaram's room."

Kuntal was still defiant. "But I didn't go to Dad's room."

Rajiv put his hands in his back pocket and pulled out a handcuff. Aprarajita and Kuntal were stunned. He flashed the handcuff and said, "Mr. Kuntal, I am arresting you for lying to a police officer. If you are not going to tell me the truth, we have ways of getting the truth out." Rajiv did not have any arrest warrant and would not have been able to arrest Kuntal, but the antics did the trick. Kuntal was cornered, and he was not in a clear state of mind to think logically. He was scared to death at the idea of a prison. He urgently kneeled down on the floor and begged Rajiv to spare him. He promised to tell the truth and began to cry.

"I will tell you the truth, Inspector; please do not arrest me, please. Yes, I did go to Dad's room to check the locker. As I said, we wanted to know how much money the locker holds, so that we could ask Dad for a reasonable sum. I did not want to steal any of it. I stealthily went to his room and opened the locker using the hint that Dad told to Sparsh. Trust me, Inspector, I did nothing more."

Before Rajiv or Kuntal could say more, Aparajita added, "Please trust us Inspector, I forced him to do it. He did not want to, but I needed to know how much Dad had in that locker. If we knew, we could ask for an appropriate amount of money as we could ask only once. We couldn't keep asking for money every time. Please Inspector, please believe us."

Rajiv only knew that Vicky had heard footsteps, around 3 am, of someone going up the stairs. It had to be Hari, Pubali, or Kuntal as they were the only ones who lived on the ground floor. Hari had already said that he did not go to Mr. Balaram's room that night as he was not called for. The chances were 50/50, but the fact that Sparsh saw his father leave bed at night made Kuntal a winner. Rajiv knew that he wouldn't get a better chance to get a confession and so he had taken his shot and it hit bull's eye.

Rajiv said, "So, around 3 am, your father's room was open and he was alive?"

"I can assure you, there were no blood wounds. He was sleeping."

"Did he snore or move?"

"No, neither of them. I didn't see him moving."

"How much money was there in the locker?"

"Nothing, it was empty."

"How can it be empty? I am sure you do understand, Mr. Kuntal, what I must be thinking."

"Trust me Inspector, please. I did not steal it. I was equally surprised, but I had no other options, so I left the room."

Aparajita also vouched for her husband. "Yes, Inspector, we are not thieves, and we did not steal it. I can swear on Sparsh, he will die if I am lying. We did not steal anything, please, please trust us," and she began crying.

"Please don't cry, Mrs. Aparajita, I believe you but you must tell me, are you hiding anything else from me?"

"No, nothing at all, I swear."

"Ok, one final thing. Mr. Kuntal, on the day when your father died, you arranged for the removal of the ventilator fan from the ventilator shaft in your father's bathroom. I know my profession makes me suspect every detail; however, don't you find it odd? The fan was having issues for 2 weeks, and you did not arrange for it to be fixed. You finally managed to do it, and that very night, your father got killed, presumably, by someone, who had entered the room through that open ventilator shaft?"

"Trust me please, Inspector, my Dad used to call me multiple times to get it fixed, as I had the carpenter's number. He called me the previous night too and bellowed at me for being a useless son. Finally, I called the carpenter and arranged it to be fixed the next day. I had no idea this could happen. I did not even know that the carpenter was going to take the fan with him. It is all a coincidence."

"Ok, I shall take your word for it, as of now. Thanks for your time but I may come back to disturb you again. As we are all confessing, I would also confess that Mr. Vicky did not see you entering the room, I made that up. He only heard someone going up the stairs." Rajiv left the bewildered couple as they just looked at each other, awestruck.

CHAPTER 14

ArpitaTalukdar

♡ ◯ ▽ ⊓

8526 likes

ArpitaTalukdar The Shetty Family already suffered the greatest loss, but still, @BangalorePolice cannot stop harassing them. They are interrogating them for 2 days. Even, Late Balaram Shetty's grandson was interviewed! What is he going to confess? That he stole Lollypops from his granddad! Why are the Police Force so inhumane? Don't they have kids at home?

#inhumanepolice #shameonBangalorePolice

#familyshouldbespared #noJusticeinIndia

View all 479 comments

2 HOURS AGO

Rajiv had taken the rest of the day off, as it was her Princess's birthday. They had planned for a big party in the evening and booked a hotel's ballroom for it. Rajiv and Devika were busy with sending invitations to everyone since the past week, but lately, due to Mr. Balaram Shetty's homicide case, Rajiv had lost focus on family duties. Judging by Rajiv's husband skills, Devika already expected him to go wrong with the invites, so she confirmed with Rajiv if he had invited everyone, that she had requested. That's when Rajiv realized that he had missed to invite three family friends but he dared not accept this. He confirmed that he has invited all of them. Once Devika was away from sight, immediately he dialed the three family friends and explained them about the complex case of Mr. Balaram Shetty that he was dealing with, which was his excuse to forget inviting them. He apologized multiple times and requested them to come but not tell Devika about this. Two of the family friends laughed it out but Manoj Kumar, who was one among those three family friends showed interest in Mr. Balaram Shetty's murder case. He kept on asking curious questions about the case. Rajiv answered a few, but when his questions would not end, he said that he will talk in details about it once Manoj came to the party in the evening.

Devika had brought a birthday dress for her daughter, Saloni. In the afternoon, both the parents went to the birthday girl's room and presented the dress to her. She liked it, but when Devika asked her to wear it and show to her parents, she refused. She took a good look at the dress, the material, and the style of it and finally voiced her opinion, "I don't want to wear this on my birthday, Mom. I want to wear what Dhriti wore on her birthday, but that same dress has to be in light blue."

Rajiv said "Who is Dhriti, and how can we know what Dhriti wore on her birthday?"

Devika gave Rajiv a withering look.

"Dad, Dhriti is my best friend, and she wore this dress on her birthday." She unlocked her phone, surfed through some pictures, and showed it to her Dad.

Rajiv had a look at it. As far as he was concerned, he only realized that it was some princess-type gown with flowers in it. He said, "Show it to your mother." Then he turned to his wife and asked, "Devika, where can we get this? That too in light blue?"

Devika was not one to pamper her child beyond limits. She knew where to draw the line, unlike her husband. She looked at the dress and said, "Darling, if you wanted to wear a specific dress on your birthday, you should have told us before we brought this dress for you. We would have given you any dress you wanted, but you should have given us a heads up. It's your mistake that you did not tell us about this before but we will try to fix it to the best we can. I cannot promise anything. You do not like this dress, then, we will go to the store where we brought it. They have a good collection; you can choose your own birthday dress form that store. That is the best we can do for you. Otherwise, you will have to wear this dress. Your choice."

Saloni knew that purring up to Mom would not be of any use, so she looked towards Dad and said, "Dad! How is this fair? Can't I even get the single thing I want for my birthday?"

Devika knew that Saloni was her husband's week point. He would do anything for her; so, she stepped in the conversation between her daughter and her husband. She commanded, "Saloni, this is not my decision; it is OUR decision. Your father already agrees with me on it, and you will go with us, right now. You will choose your birthday dress from that store. That is final. Get dressed up. We are leaving in 15 minutes. There are a lot of arrangements pending for the party." Had Devika not used that particular tone in her last statement, or command, however you want to interpret it, Rajiv would presently be scavenging the entire market for his princess's birthday dress. However, Rajiv and Saloni both had realized that Devika's decree shall stand and they must follow it. So, no use arguing about it.

That evening, there were around 200 guests for Saloni's birthday party. Three quarters of that were Saloni's friends and their family. Rajiv and Saloni had decided that they would not invite their office colleague, as the place cannot hold a bigger audience, it may get crowded. Still, immediate seniors in office cannot be avoided. So, both of them invited only their immediate seniors.

Saloni had selected a blue princess gown as her birthday dress, but it did not have any flowers on it. She looked stunning in it and was happy about it too. There was a live DJ and a young crowd, most of them on the dance floor and others at the mocktail counter. Rajiv wanted a cocktail counter, but Devika convinced him for a mocktail. She promised that once Saloni passed her 12th board exams and went to college, they will have a cocktail counter instead of a mocktail one. However, Rajiv was not one to lose a debate without managing to win something from it. He convinced Devika for a hookah counter along with the mocktail counter. The hookah counter was a super hit. Saloni's friends loved it, and so did Rajiv's boss.

Midway through the party, Mr. Manoj caught Rajiv at the Mock tail counter, and after a few minutes of soft chat, enquired about Mr. Balaram's murder. Rajiv was in no mood to talk shop and kept avoiding the topic, but Mr. Manoj kept insisting on details. At that time, Rajiv's senior also came to the mocktail counter for a drink and got engaged in the conversation. He asked about all the findings so far in the case. Rajiv laughed it out and ignored it. He confirmed to his senior that he would give a full report about the case, first thing tomorrow morning but for now, he requested him to enjoy the drinks and the food. Fortunately, at this time, Saloni came to his rescue and pulled him for a dance. As soon as Saloni brought Devika and Rajiv to the dance floor, everyone stepped out to give the dance floor to the family. Both the parents got embarrassed, but others kept insisting for a family dance. The DJ even changed the song to a remix 'Hum Saath Saath Hein' version, which made it more difficult to dance. Finally, the beautiful family of three danced together for barely a minute while everyone clapped. Though it was embarrassing, that minute was one of the best minute in Rajiv's life. He looked up and thanked God for blessing him with such a lovely family.

CHAPTER 15

Arvind Chatterjee

2 h

My friends and I are organizing a peaceful candle march from **@Lalbagh Botanical Garden** at 2 pm, 3 March. The candle march will be to pay our respects to Late Chief Justice Balaram Shetty and to protest against **@Bangalore Police** who are yet clueless about the murderer. Please spread this message so that anyone else who is interested can join us. Our strength is in our Unity

#CandleMarch #2pm3March

#UselessBangalorePolice

#Justice4Justice

9k Likes 1953 Comments 583 Shares

India 4Life

@india4life

The murder mystery of Late Honorable Justice Balaram Shetty keeps on dragging. No arrests made yet. How will there be arrests if @iamRajivBakshi is busy partying! YES, you heard it right, @iamRajivBakshi was pictured dancing and cheering at a party while we wait for Justice.

#replaceRajivBakshi #chiefjusticeneedsjustice

1:08 PM · Mar 2, 2020 ·Twitter Web App

6940 Retweet **7423** Comment **11546** Likes

The Police Commissioner called Rajiv while he was reading the newspaper. He slammed, "Have you read Page 6 of the newspaper. How does the press have photos of you dancing in a party? How can you dance and laugh when you have such a big case on your hands? You have not taken a step forward to resolve the case, and you are still partying? Do you know how many questions are being asked about our Police force in social media? Stupid hashtags about our ineptness are trending on social media. I want you to resolve this case as soon as possible, Rajiv, otherwise I will have to take strict action against you."

Rajiv tried to explain how his personal life should have been separate from his professional life, but the Police Commissioner had already hung up. Rajiv cursed the Press and hashtags aloud and cursed the Commissioner inaudibly.

Back at the police station, Rajiv was drumming on his head in his office, trying to comprehend all the facts of the case. The most important piece of the puzzle has to be the post mortem report, and he called Mr. Dhole to get a status report on that.

When the havildar asked Mr. Dhole to go to Rajiv's cabin, his heart pounded. From his past experiences with Rajiv, Mr. Dhole assumed that he must have done something wrong. He re-checked all the facts of the case, trying to find out what he might have missed, but he could not find anything. He looked towards the ceiling, prayed to God, and knocked on Rajiv's cabin. It was evident that Rajiv was not happy about something. When Mr. Dhole came to know why he was called, he was most surprised, as Rajiv had called him to take his advice. Rajiv said, "I need your help. I know I am missing something in this case. Can we go over the facts again please?"

Mr. Dhole's chest pumped. "Yes Sir, let's do it; I would be happy to help."

"Where are we with the post mortem report?"

"It should be with us at 7 pm tomorrow."

"Tell me again, when did you come to know about the murder? When did you reach Kunj Villa? What did you do till I reached there?"

"I got a call at the police station at around 20 minutes past 10 in the morning, and I immediately made my way to Kunj Villa, along with the team. We reached there by quarter to 11 and immediately sealed off Mr. Balaram's room. We asked basic questions to all the family members. All of them said that the last time they saw Mr. Balaram was at breakfast the previous morning. Only the servant, Hari, had seen Mr. Balaram alive and healthy at 11 pm that night, when he went to get the dinner plates from Mr. Balaram's room. We confirmed from everyone that none of them touched or misplaced anything in Mr. Balaram's room. As per protocol, we did a thorough search of all the other rooms in the house but found nothing suspicious. We took everyone's finger prints and then you came in."

"What did Mr. Balaram have for dinner? Can we rule out poison in that food?"

"Not till we have the Autopsy report, Sir. He had a sabji, daal, and roti. However, Hari said that he served the same menu from the same casserole to others in the house too. So, I think we can rule that out."

"What were you searching for in everyone's room?"

"Standard protocol, sir, anything suspicious. The murder weapon was clearly a knife, which we did not find in Mr. Balaram's room. Therefore, we were searching for a bloody knife or anything sharp. We were also looking for any hidden cash stacked anywhere. We looked everywhere; we even carved open the sofa and bed but did not find anything major. Every family had some cash, but those were in thousands. We checked for blood traces in all the sharp items in the kitchen but could not find anything."

"Did you search inside Sparsh's dolls?"

"No, sir, that we did not but why are you asking? Do you think Mr. Kuntal has something to do with it?"

"As I see it, everyone in that house is a primary suspect. I tricked Mr. Kuntal into confessing that he went to Mr. Balaram's room at around 3 am. He wanted to loot the locker in Mr. Balaram's room. He opened the locker but found it to be empty. I am not sure if he is telling the truth."

Mr. Dhole got angry. "What! That son of a bitch was hiding it from us! I will go and teach him a lesson. Did he check if Mr. Balaram was alive at that time?"

"He said that he saw no blood."

Rajiv took a pause and then resumed. "Have we opened the locker? Did we find any cash inside it?"

"Yes, sir, we opened the locker but there was no cash in it. The code was...."

"556696, I know."

"How, sir?" Exclaimed Mr. Dhole.

"Mr. Kuntal used his son to get a hint from his Dad about the locker pass code, and Mr. Balaram said that his family is the pass code. There are 6 living members of his family, except him. If we arrange the number of letters in each name, in an age wise descending order, you have the pass code."

"That's very smart of you, sir."

"Even that dumbass Kuntal, who fell into my trap, could solve it. Therefore, I do not think there is any smartness to it. The oldies are never complex with passwords and, most of all, hints. However, I think Mrs. Aparajita solved the password; that lady is shrewd."

"So, he was alive at 3 am and the door was open?"

"Looks like it. In addition, we do not have the murder weapon or the cash. Can you check for fingerprints on the locker and see if you can find anything there? May be that will tell us who took the cash!"

"I had already requested that; the report should be with us any moment now."

Mr. Dhole continued, "I looked into the case of Mrs. Sabitri's suicide, as you ordered. She killed herself with a kitchen knife; it was found next to her, and it had her fingerprints on it."

"If it's a kitchen knife, there must be other fingerprints too. Did we find any other fingerprints?"

"Yes, the police found Hari's fingerprints too, but as it was a kitchen knife, it was supposed to have his fingerprints."

"Did you get photos of that murder scene? I need to see them."

"Yes, sir, here you go." Mr. Dhole was well prepared this time, as he had the photos handy.

Rajiv examined the photos. "The stab marks are deep. Using a kitchen knife, it would take a lot of strength to go this deep inside the belly. When you are harming yourself, your body would resist in pulling up additional strength, and if a woman has to do it to herself, she has to be in good physical and mental shape, which was not the case here. How did the police judge this as suicide?"

Mr. Dhole looked at the photos. "I agree with you, sir, but this is derivative evidence. This will not sustain in court, and they must have had a lot of pressure from above, as the case was high profile. The only suspect in the case was Mr. Ronit, and if they had to arrest him on murder charges, they had to put a strong case, which they did not have. So, it's a suicide. Win-win for everyone."

"I do not like this attitude, Mr. Dhole. I understand that you are being practical, but it was not a win for our police force. We were only subdued, and we should be ashamed of it."

"Apologies, sir."

"So, if we are thinking that Mr. Ronit could have killed his own wife, then he can kill his Dad too. He was pissed about his Dad spilling the truth about his affair to Mrs. Sabitri. He could have taken revenge. If we are to assume that he had stabbed before, he can stab now too. That makes him a strong suspect. Mr. Dhole, have you got the phone history of all the members of the family?"

Finally, Mr. Dhole's fears came true; he did miss a standard protocol. "No, sir, not yet; I will get it as soon as possible."

"You told me that you followed all standard protocol! Then how did you miss this? In today's digital age, phone records solve most of the crimes. I want all of their phone records before the autopsy report. Is it clear?"

A shivering Mr. Dhole answered in the affirmative.

"Check Mr. Ronit's phone records to see if he is still having the affair with that girl from his office. Maybe that is why he murdered his wife. We can get some leads from there."

Mr. Dhole was desperate to change the topic, "What about the oldest son, Mr. Vicky? I have already told you about the molestation case he was involved in, but again, we could not get evidence. Did Mr. Vicky tell anything about that case?"

"No, I did not ask about it yet; we shall use it when the time comes. Where are we with the fingerprints on the cigarette butt?"

"It should be with us tomorrow morning, sir."

"Mr. Vicky is the only one who left the house on that morning. That too for a morning stroll! Someone who never goes for a stroll. I am sure he is up to something, and we need to get it out of him. He is hiding something. Actually, everyone in the house looks to be hiding something. I can sense it."

"Rajiv sir, did anyone say anything else which might be useful for us?"

"Ronit said he heard a female voice from Dad's room, but he can't be sure of it, and Vicky said he thinks there was someone at the corridor or Mr. Balaram's room at around 2 am, but he can't be exactly sure."

"If it's a lady's voice, it has to be either Mrs. Pubali or Mrs. Aparajita."

Rajiv said, "I asked you to check about Mrs. Pubali's divorce case. What is the status?"

"I followed up on the case, and it looks like the case is swaying towards her husband. Evidence suggests that Mrs. Pubali never wanted to settle down in her married life. She left her husband within the first 3 months and lived separately. There is no evidence of physical abuse. The neighbors have testified that Mrs. Pubali never showed respect to her in-laws; she smoked and drank whisky in front of them. The neighbors also testified that she would get drunk and shout at her husband and her in-laws but no one testified anything about the in-laws or the husband shouting back. The husband's lawyer is alleging that she only married him so that she can get a divorce and the alimony. She is demanding 70 lakhs of alimony, but if she loses the case, she will not get a penny."

"What were Mr. Balaram's views on this?"

"He had reportedly told the media that he blamed himself for Mrs. Pubali's actions, and he sincerely apologized to her in-laws on her behalf. He did not support her daughter on this, but Mrs. Pubali still pursued on with the divorce case."

"What kind of twisted family is this? Isn't anyone normal here?"

After a pause, Rajiv questioned again, "What about the people whom Mr. Balaram had sentenced? Did you check on that line?"

"Yes, sir; among the prisoners sentenced by Mr. Balaram, only 5 prisoners have been released over the last 2 years."

"Ok, who are they and what is their profile?"

"First one is a thief, Raju. He was sentenced for 10 years for trying to loot a bank. He has found some stable work in Pune and shifted there, around a year ago."

"Ok, let's ignore him as of now. Next?"

Mr. Dhole pulled up another file. "Rashika Dulai, sentenced for 14 years imprisonment for murder of her husband. You mentioned this woman. She is still in Bangalore, release from jail, 8 months ago."

Rajiv instructed, "Do a background check and ask her to come for an interrogation."

"Ok, next is Tariq Masoom, sentenced for 10 years from blackmailing charges. He was released 18 months ago and presently settled in Chandigarh, recently married to a girl there."

Rajiv asked to move on to the next one.

"Srinivas M, sentenced for 8 years on a domestic violence case and released 3 months ago. He has returned to his home town in Kerala and added his profile on Bharat Matrimony."

"Next?"

"Vikas Kumar, the one you enquired about. He is in Bangalore, released 4 months ago."

"Arrange a meeting with him."

Before Mr. Dhole could answer, his phone rang, and he excused himself to pick it up. As soon as he dropped the call, he excitedly turned towards Rajiv and said, "The finger prints from the locker are here, and guess whose fingerprints they found!"

CHAPTER 16

Daring Darling

@daredal

I just now got a message from a friend that a Candle March Protest is organized from Lalbagh Botanical Garden at 2 pm, tomorrow, 3 March. This peaceful protest is to demand justice for the respected late Chief Justice Balaram Shetty. I am definitely going. Hope to see you all there. Also, please share this message to others, so that it can reach the ears and eyes of young Indians. @BangalorePolice must know that the youth of India will not sit quietly and wait for Justice, we will GET IT.

#IstandforBalaramShetty #shameonRajiv #shameonBangPolice #candledrive #protestismybirthright#Justice4Justice

7:47 PM · Mar 2, 2020 ·Twitter Web App

1897 Retweet **1265** Comment **2875** Likes

By afternoon, Mr. Dhole had the phone records of everyone in Mr. Balaram's house. Rajiv instructed Mr. Dhole to match the numbers with their criminal database. As soon as Mr. Dhole ran the numbers through the database, they hit pay dirt. Ramadas Kumar, aka Bihari. A petty criminal, who served jail, multiple times. He wasn't a murderer, at least he was never charged for a murder, yet. However, he had been charged with robbery, narcotics, illegal arms possession, and cutting two fingers of one of his gang members. This was a progressive finding for the case, as police has leverage over anyone with a criminal history, and they fit well with a murder case. Mr. Dhole wanted to arrest Bihari immediately, but surprisingly, Rajiv denied his request.

Rajiv was one of the toppers in his school life, and he did well in higher studies too. While his friends dreaded homework, Rajiv was fanatical about it. He always believed that homework was the most critical element of success, as it tested your knowledge about what you have learnt and helped you to channel that in exams. He did not let go this mantra in professional life too. He always did his homework before any interrogation or investigation. For Mr. Balaram's case, when he was assigned the murder case, he was an hour late to come to Kunj Villa. During this time, he was doing a background study of Mr. Balaram and his family through his sources. This is how Rajiv worked. Therefore, in case of Bihari, he did not sign off his immediate arrest. Instead, he asked Mr. Dhole to track the mobile location of Bihari on the night of the murder and check if the footprint they had from Kunj Villa matched with the size of Bihari's shoe.

On the other hand, since his childhood, Mr. Dhole had been someone who got his homework done by his sister or friends. He was not an admirer of exams but believed in actions rather than preparations. He used all standard cheating protocols, like copying notes on the back of calculator, hollowing out pens to hide secret notes and others to pass the exam. Therefore, he seldom appreciated Rajiv's method. He believed he could slap the truth out of Bihari, but seniority had the ultimate hand, so, he had fewer options than to comply. He quickly paced his way through Rajiv's instructions. When he had those records, he could finally do it his way. All criminals can hide from police until the time that the police needs to find him. When that time comes, the police force is surprisingly efficient, and anyone can be found and arrested within 24 hours. It took Mr. Dhole two hours to bring Bihari to the police station, and within the evening, Rajiv was interrogating Bihari.

A further hour more, Rajiv had Bihari trapped, because Rajiv had done his homework. The more Bihari lied, the more Rajiv got the upper hand in the interrogation when he busted his lies with proof, and finally, Bihari confessed.

Mr. Dhole congratulated Rajiv for getting to the truth, but Rajiv said, "Talking about truth, we need to find out what are those siblings hiding. I am sure they are hiding something; we need to quickly find out what they are hiding. That is the key to this case. I can feel it."

"But how, sir? We can't beat it out of them."

"We hurt him where they are weak; that's how."

"Where are they weak?" Mr. Dhole asked innocently.

Rajiv just looked up at Mr. Dhole and said, "You don't need to stress your brains on it. I will break them tomorrow. They will spill out the truth. I just need another session with Bihari. I will be right back." After half an hour, Rajiv returned from the interrogation with a smirk on his face.

Around an hour later, Mr. Dhole informed Rajiv that Vikas Kumar and Rashika Dulai were here for interrogation, as Rajiv had asked. Rajiv urged to arrange for seating them in different rooms.

As the 'Ladies First' rule dictates, Rajiv attended to Mrs. Rashika Dulai first. Rajiv put his sights on a women of about 55 years, her skinny bones portraying starvation, cheeks wrinkled, skin color faded by constant torture of life and eyes sunken by grief. She looked to be someone living in mercy of the nature. Rajiv's heart broke for her.

Before taking a seat, Rajiv called a havildar and asked for two cups of tea and some biscuits. "How are you doing Mrs. Dulai? My name is Rajiv Bakshi, and I would like to ask you a few questions, is that fine?"

Rajiv wasn't expecting a revolt from such a poor creature, but he couldn't be right every time. She rebuked in Hindi, which translated to – 'That is something you should have asked before dragging me here. I know what this is about. I am happy that asshole is dead. I even cried from joy when I heard about it. Unfortunately, I did not have anything to do with it. Someone else stole my chance to provide some closure to my daughter.'

The conversation followed in Hindi then onwards.

“It appears that you desperately wanted Justice Balaram Shetty dead!”

“I would have made sure that he is dead but as I said, someone stole that opportunity from me.”

“Where were you on the night of the murder?”

“From 10 pm to midnight, I was outside Kunj Villa. After that, I went to my home, which is an hour away from Kunj Villa. Therefore, I reached my house around 1 am, had my dinner with Archana, my neighbor. After that, I went to sleep. Next morning, I heard the good news.”

Rajiv was surprised by the composed admissions of Mrs. Rashika Dulai. He felt like he was losing the ground in this interrogation. Mrs. Dulai was confessing everything but also keeping herself out of the equation.

“What were you doing outside Kunj Villa?”

“Surveillance. I wanted to kill that bastard judge, and I was figuring out his time table. I have been watching him for that whole week, trying to figure out how I can murder him.” The arrogance and boldness of Mrs. Dulai was alarming, like she had nothing to lose.

Rajiv countered, “You have the motive, and you have yourself mentioned that you were around Kunj Villa. So tell me, why should I not arrest you on suspicion of murder?'

“Because, though God has deprived me of revenge, but he has also taken care to provide me with multiple alibis, which can confirm that I was in my house at the time of the murder. Otherwise, useless police officers like you would falsely arrest us without any proof, and wipe their hands off the duty to find the actual murderer. I took a bus from Kunj Villa that night; the bus driver can vouch for me. It was my neighbor's birthday that night. She was outside her house, with some friends, when I reached home. I went ahead and wished her. She welcomed me to her home; we had cake and snacks and chatted about our grief till 2 am. So, there is no way you can prove my connection to that asshole's murder."

Rajiv dithered to question further but before he could speak, she asked rudely if the interrogation was over and if she could leave now? Rajiv conceded defeat and nodded acceptance.

As Rajiv came out of the interview room, Mr. Dhole was expectantly waiting outside, like a 'would be' father waits outside the operation theatre. As soon as Mr. Dhole saw Rajiv, with a certain degree of edginess in his voice, he asked about the operation, hoping to hear good news. Rajiv shrugged and moved to the next interrogation room. Mr. Dhole assumed from the vocal silence and loud thudding of Rajiv's footsteps that it did not go well.

Working under the Indian Police Department had taught Rajiv how to accept dominion from the higher management, but nothing had prepared him to face a strong and determined character as Mrs. Rashika Dulai. Rajiv had judged the book by its cover and was jolted to find what was inside. He might have assumed submissiveness from Mrs. Rashika's background, which was a big mistake. He just couldn't come to terms with how he was dominated by Mrs. Rashika, and he was pissed and determined to not make the same mistake again with Vikas Kumar.

As Rajiv entered the room where Vikas Kumar was seated, he folded his sleeves and took a seat. His body language and tone was much more aggressive than usual. He let go of his usual style of interrogation to trap the person in their own web of lies. Instead, he went directly for the kill.

Rajiv shouted on the top of his voice, "Son of a bitch, tell me right now, why the fuck did you murder Balaram Shetty? Tell me or I am going to piss the truth out of you."

Vikas had already been through many interrogations due to his past mischief and replied like a PRO, in a calm and mocking voice, "What are you saying, sir? So direct! Shouldn't you be first asking me for tea and then start with where I was on that night, what is my alibi, and then try to prove me wrong? Personally, I think that would be more fruitful for you rather than such direct questions. However, looks like you are in a hurry to go over this interview, so let's get it done with. My answer would be that I did not murder that asshole Balaram Shetty, and I was at a friend's place that night. My friend can verify it too. Now, is the interview over? Can I leave?"

As usual, there were cameras recording the interview, and other police officers listening to the interview from outside. As Police officers are violence-shy in front of cameras, this does not seldom happen, but Rajiv sulked his face towards the left, gave a wicked smile, murmured some words, and in an instant, pounced on Vikas Kumar, punching and kicking him in rage. He shouted at the top of his voice, "If you are innocent, then why did you come prepared with an alibi, you piece of shit? CONFESS, CONFESS right now."

It must have been 15 odd seconds before other police officers rushed to the room, and two police officers pulled Rajiv out of the fight. Vikas's face was bleeding heavily, and he was stunned by the sudden unexpected attack. One of the police officers quickly stopped the video recording, pulled out the memory card out, and put it in his pockets.

Every officer knew that what had happened was not legal or appropriate, and they restrained a panting Rajiv from getting near to Vikas, but Mr. Dhole did not want to waste the momentum. Anyway, there were no cameras anymore, so, no holds barred. Vikas was still down on the floor and bleeding. Mr. Dhole picked him up, threatened to hit him again, and asked, "Tell us the truth, RIGHT NOW. Why did you kill him?"

The person who had been a shrewd criminal few moments ago was crying like a baby now and shaking with fear. "Trust me Sir, I did not kill him. I wanted to; I wanted to hurt him and his family members but never thought of killing him. I even asked one of my punters to find out where and when we could attack, but the old man never left his home. Therefore, we were just waiting for our chance, but we never hurt him. We never got a chance. Trust me, sir, please trust me."

In between this time, Rajiv had regained his poise. He realized the situation and urged Mr. Dhole to continue with further questioning, end it quickly, arrange for his treatment, and pay some compensation. Rajiv needed to cool down and reconvene himself, so he left the interrogation room, leaving Mr. Dhole in charge.

CHAPTER 17

ArpitaTalukdar

♡ ◯ ▽ ◻

2769 likes

ArpitaTalukdar

Candles – Check

Banners – Check

Boards – Check

Passion – Double Check

Ready for the candle march today. Let's make it a success.

#candlemarch #ProtestIWill #shameonBangalorePolice

#fightforJustice #Justice4Justice

View all 653 comments

3 HOURS AGO

Next morning, Rajiv triumphantly entered Kunj Villa along with Mr. Dhole. He asked Hari for a cup of tea and requested him to ask everyone to join him in the dining area. Hari sprinted away to make tea. Mr. Dhole looked up at Rajiv with questioning eyes but Rajiv only signaled him to be patient. Soon, everyone ramblingly gathered and gestured with questioning eyes towards Rajiv and one another. Rajiv asked them all to be seated, as he had some major announcements.

As Rajiv sipped in his cup of tea, he looked up and said, "I will be frank with all of you. When I got this case and started the investigation, I was sure it was an inside job. I could put my money on it that someone from the house had murdered Mr. Balaram. I know how wrong it sounds, but you cannot blame me for it. If you were in my shoes, you would have done the same. I hope all of you understand."

Rajiv gave a pause and everyone affirmatively hummed.

"I must apologize to all of you for that, and all the wrong words I may have said to any of you, as I was just doing my investigation. Now that we have found the guilty party, I feel mortified to have troubled all of you like that."

"You found our father's killer? Who is it?" questioned Vicky.

"Mr. Dhole, bring him in," ordered Rajiv.

Mr. Dhole left the house and dragged a five-feet-five-inch rugged man, whose hands were handcuffed and face was covered with a black cloth. Everyone was in awe.

"Who is this? Did he kill our father?" asked Pubali.

"We can only give out his name to all of you after we declare this in the press conference. I just wanted to let you know so that you do not have to learn about it from the media. Moreover, of course, I wanted to apologize to all of you. Mr. Dhole, please take him away."

"How did you find him? Why did he kill our father?" enquired Kuntal.

"We traced him using the footprint we found in the lawn. Unfortunately, for him, he selected a rainy night to commit this unthinkable crime. He is a petty criminal, and Mr. Balaram had sentenced him to 5 years of imprisonment for a theft. He was recently out, after serving his jail time. We think that it is related to revenge, but we can say something concrete only after the interrogation is completed."

"Thank you, Inspector, by when will this interrogation be over so that we can press charges? We want the strongest charges against him," said Ronit.

"Mr. Ronit, talking about interrogation, I apologize if I had used some strong words during your interrogation. You must understand you were my primary suspect, as you have a history of killing someone."

Ronit was staggered. "History of Killing! Me! What do you mean, Inspector?"

Rajiv faked innocence. "I mean the case of your wife, Mrs Sabitri. Your brother, Mr. Kuntal told me during his interrogation that she was 'killed'. I assumed you would have killed her and got away with it, as you were the only one with motive."

Ronit's eyes turned red, and he shouted at Kuntal, "Did you say this, you bastard?"

Kuntal was taken aback. "What are you saying, Inspector? When did I say it?"

Rajiv was calm. "We have faced this many a times. People confess something during the interrogation and later on go ahead to deny it, as the truth does not suit them well. For this kind of scenarios, as per standard protocol, we always record each interrogation with any suspect. Wait a minute."

Rajiv took out his mobile, surfed for around two minutes to enact that he was unprepared for this, and he was searching for the appropriate recording. Once the sufficient delay had been enacted, he played a part of the recording where Kuntal could be clearly heard saying, *'Police is nothing new to Sparsh. About an year ago, when Sabitri Bhabhi was killed, the police stormed the house and kept coming for days and interrogated everyone, just like now.'*

Kuntal leaped up. "I did not mean it like that. I meant it's a suicide, but it came out wrong, trust me Ronit Bhaiya."

Rajiv again pitched in. "I thought you killed Mrs. Sabitri for your affair with your office colleague."

Rajiv then turned towards Kuntal and said, "What was the name of that lady, Mr. Kuntal, which you told us? I can't remember it."

Ronit was fuming at his brother. "You told this too!"

Rajiv said, "As I said, I have recordings. I can play it."

Ronit was the hothead of the family. He had a history of brawls with his siblings, especially when he was angry. Now, he was angry. "You bastard, you call yourself a brother, you backstabbing bitch!" In his rage, Ronit rushed towards Kuntal to hit him.

Mr. Dhole rushed to stop the tussle, but Rajiv signaled him not to.

The other members of the house joined to separate the two brothers, who were already throwing blows at one another.

Ronit already had both of his hands around his brother's neck, choking Kuntal. Vicky and Pubali were pulling Ronit out of the fight, and Aparajita desperately tried to free Ronit's grip on her husband's neck. Kuntal was frantic to grab a breath, but the grip was still strong. Ronit angrily shouted, "*Chutiye*, You wanted me to rot in jail so that I do not get a share of Dad's properties, and you have more for yourself! Dad already gave you and your stupid son more share in the property! How much more do you want, fucker?"

Rajiv signaled Mr. Dhole to stop the fight. Mr. Dhole rushed to the scene and, like a professional bouncer, dragged Ronit out of the fight. Ronit was still raging and ranting. Rajiv went towards Ronit and tried to calm him down."Do you think Kuntal did it for the property share? Really? But as there is no will of Mr. Balaram, the property share will be equal, isn't it?"

In ideal senses, Ronit would have answered that differently. Others even signaled him to skip the question, but a man who has just been pulled out of a raging fist fight is never in his senses. "*Bhosdike ko jyada mila hein*. He has received more property share than us, and we are only left with freaking five lakhs each. He has fifteen lakhs because he has a fucking son. Can you imagine this? Still he wants more! That too at the cost of his own brother?"

Everyone paced forward to shut Ronit's mouth and rage, but Mr. Dhole stopped them all. Rajiv turned Ronit's face away from the others and said to him, "Don't worry, nothing like that will happen. There is no official will by which this can be enforced; you are mistaken. It must be a bad dream."

"Bad dream my ass, how can there be an official will? Dad got killed before he could make it official. He was supposed to make it official the next day."

"But you brothers cannot have five lakhs each; there is a lot more money that needs to be distributed in the will. Your father must not have checked his bank account properly before making this will."

"No, that old fucker was disappointed with us, with what we have turned out to be, so he wrote a cheque of 60 lakhs for donation. That's how he wanted to teach us a lesson. He even fucking signed the cheque the night of his birthday, in front of us. Can you imagine! And we call him a father!"

Rajiv loosened his grip on Ronit's shoulders and tapped him to calm down and have some water. He triumphantly looked at the rest of the audience. Mr. Dhole looked amazed, while others were finding places to sulk and hide their face.

Rajiv addressed everyone now. "I knew all of you were hiding something. All of you were hiding your motive to kill your father, and finally, it is out. The truth will always find its way. Sometimes, through crooked ways, as that's how you deal with criminals. All of you are criminals now, as you have officially lied to police during its investigation. I am going to press charges against all of you, and you will rot in jail."

The threat of jail term was enough to calm down Ronit. While for others, it was their nightmare. Everyone pleaded with folded hands, apologized to Rajiv, and said, "We knew how bad it looked, sir; we knew the situation was against us. Our father was dead the night he seized 60 lakhs from us, and it would make us look like murderers. Therefore, we jointly decided to hide that. No one else apart from us knew about this. We will tell you everything now, but please do not take us to jail."

"Tell me everything that happened that night."

The family members briefed about the night to Rajiv and Mr. Dhole in detail. Then Aparajita said, "I know that this makes us suspects for the case, but we really do not know where the cheque for 60 lakhs or the papers for the will are. As you already know, we did not have anything to do with his murder. It is just a coincidence that the filthy black hooded person you brought here murdered our Dad the same night that all of this happened."

Rajiv grinned triumphantly, "When did I mention that person murdered your father?"

Aparajita was stunned. "What are you saying, sir, it was the first thing you said. It is the reason you came here today."

"I think you must be mistaken, Mrs. Aparajita. As I said earlier, all our conversations are recorded, and I can replay the recording of whatever I said today. I never said he was your father's murderer. That would be lying. I only mentioned that this person admitted to his guilt. He is guilty of trespassing on Kunj Villa on the night of the murder. His footprints were found in the lawn, but I never mentioned he is the murderer. All of you assumed that."

All the audience was aghast. "How can you do that Inspector. You deceived us!" asked Ronit.

Rajiv patted Ronit on the shoulder and said, "Just like you were deceiving the police force and hiding this from me! Anyways, thanks for the truth, we will continue our investigation."

Rajiv turned to Pubali and said, "Mrs. Pubali, we need to have some word, can we go to your room please?"

CHAPTER 18

Arvind Chatterjee

57 m

Today, our candle march was a great success. More than 3k protesters gathered and paid our tributes to Late Balaram Shetty. Thanks for all your support. **@Bangalore Police** you did not need to arrange for RAF, we always meant a peaceful protest. But if we do not get Justice, even RAF won't be enough, the next time we meet.

#CandleMarch #Feelsgood #PeacefulProtesters

#UselessBangalorePolice #Justice4Justice

16k Likes 1254 Comments 894 Shares

As they moved to Pubali's room, Rajiv enquired, "The man whom we showed to all of you today, the one whose foot print matches with the ones in the garden, do you know him?"

Mrs. Pubali politely responded, "His face was not visible, Inspector. I could not see him."

"How long will you play this game with us, Mrs. Shetty?"

"I did not understand. Why would I lie to you?"

Rajiv faced upwards and raised his hands in the air in despair. "Did someone come to meet you on the night of the murder?"

Pubali fumbled. "No, Inspector. Who will come to meet me at night?"

"Ok, Mrs. Shetty; let me place my cards on the table, and I hope you will do the same. The person we brought to your house just now, whom we suspect of murder, has confessed that he came to Kunj Villa that night, around 2.30 am. He also confessed that you gave him two lakh rupees that night."

Pubali was still quiet. Rajiv paused but when she did not pitch in, Rajiv continued, "So, if we add what we know till now, a felonious person deviously entered Kunj Villa and is suspected of murdering your father but that person does not have any personal agenda with Mr. Balaram. Just before your father's murder, this person received two lakh rupees in cash, from you. If I present this in court, a good lawyer may wriggle you out of the obvious by putting up an absurd story, but think about what your family will think if I tell them this. No lawyer can fix that, and with a murder case running on yourself, you would surely lose your divorce case too."

Rajiv had Pubali's unwilling attention but still, she was a spiteful one, who would fight till her last breath. "Then why don't you tell this to all of my family? What's stopping you? Why are you telling this to me personally?"

Rajiv said, "Let's be calm, Mrs. Shetty. I can easily get the truth out of that wretched crook whom we brought here today. It would take me five minutes, and he would be blabbing the whole deal to me. However, I want something else. I want that you and your brothers trust me and tell me the truth. I want to know what happened that night. I know all of you are shielding the truth from me so that you do not become a suspect. I assure you, if you did not kill your father, which I believe you did not, you will not be framed for it. However, your truth can help me nab the actual murderer. Don't you want that? Then please help me; please tell me what happened that night. I promise you, I will not judge you."

Rajiv had already cornered Pubali, but her ego was still getting in the way. With Rajiv pleading for her help, that ego got its due respect and stepped out of the way. Win-win for everyone. Finally, Pubali softened her stance. "Ok, Inspector, I will tell you the truth. I had no hands in my father's murder, and I do not have anything to hide. What I did is not 100% legal, and so I had shielded it from you initially. You must already know that I am losing my divorce case. Everyone thinks I am a gold digger and I only married to get the alimony. Even my Dad thought alike. No one understands that I am just not compatible with my husband or my in laws. Why would I keep on compromising throughout my life when I already know that he is not the right man for me and I will never be happy with him? That's why I filed for divorce, but apparently, as per Indian penal code, compatibility is not a serious enough reason for divorce. The court keeps on asking me if I got physically abused, or if I am not satisfied sexually, or if my husband is having an affair! Why would I need those reasons for a divorce? Why can't I divorce him because I do not want to be with him?"

Pubali paused to wipe her tears, but Rajiv stayed quite. "When I told the judge that I want to divorce my husband for compatibility, the judge did not allow any alimony! Can you believe it? Without alimony, how am I supposed to survive? This man married me; doesn't he have any responsibility towards me? He just wants to leave me penniless and without any financial strings attached. He thinks he can get away from me that easy! You tell me, Inspector, is this fair? Doesn't he have any responsibility towards me and my future?"

God knows that if the situation was an open debate, Rajiv would have had a lot to say, but here, a strong assertion was mandatory to keep the ball rolling, and Rajiv did likewise.

"So, I was left with no other choice than to prove that my husband is having an affair, and that is the reason for divorce. I could push for as much as 60 lakhs as alimony if I could prove that he was having an affair and he was cheating on me. However, my husband does not even have a 'female' friend, leave alone a girlfriend. Therefore, I had hired a conman, Mr. Bihari, to forge evidence that my husband was having an affair.

Bihari planned to hire some slut, get my husband drunk, and get nude pics of my husband and the slut. Typical Bollywood cliché, but it works."

Pubali turned to face Rajiv to check if he was judging her, but Rajiv maintained his poker face. "Bihari called me around 10 pm that night and confirmed that he has found a girl who would take up the job, but it needed to be done within the next 7 days as the girl would leave for Goa with another party next week. Bihari asked for two lakhs in cash immediately so that they could lay the trap but I did not have that kind of money on me. However, at midnight, when Dad called all of us to the drawing room and confirmed that he would give me five lakh rupees, as I did not use any of his cars, I jumped with joy. I promised to myself that I would turn the 5 lakhs to 60 lakhs. Around 2 am, I went to Dad's room, wished him on his birthday, and asked him for the five lakh rupees he promised. I told him that I need it as I am too stressed with the divorce case, I urgently need a long break, and I am going to book a Europe trip the day after."

Finally, Rajiv spoke. "How did he look like? Was he tensed, upset?"

"His expression? It was like he was disappointed with all of the things that were going on."

"Ok, so did he give you all the money?"

"He opened his locker and checked and told me that he only has four lakhs in cash at the moment, which he could give me. I wanted the total amount, but I urgently needed two lakhs, so I told him that he should not empty the locker, as he might need money anytime, and I could do with two lakhs today to book the trip. I could take the rest of it the next day or the day after."

"And what did he say?"

"He smiled and gave me the two lakhs. I immediately called Bihari and told him to come to Kunj Villa and take the cash. He came over soon. Through the lawn, he came to my window, took the cash at the window, and left. This is the truth, all of it."

"Is this the same window, just below Mr. Balaram's washroom, where the pipes come down to? "

"Yes, Inspector."

"Ok, that would explain the footsteps in the lawn, leading to the pipe. Thanks, Mrs. Shetty, for your co-operation. I was right to presume that you did not have anything to do with your father's murder. Can you tell me if you and your father discussed anything else that night?"

"No, nothing much, he complained that due to all the commotion that happened in the drawing room, and he was not able to sleep and asked for one of my sleeping pills. I went to my room and got him one, and then I went to my room."

"Anything more!"

"No, nothing, Inspector. This is the complete truth."

Rajiv knew it was the truth, as it matched with Bihari's confession, so he thanked Pubali and left Kunj Villa.

Rajiv approached Mr. Dhole and asked him to keep a look out on the behavior of the family members, as they had successfully cornered them today and got the truth out. He also mentioned that he would take the rest of the day off as he had some urgent family duty to attend.

CHAPTER 19

India 4Life

@india4life

4 days gone, only 1 arrest made and that too, that person has been released. What the fuck is @BangalorePolice up to? Case should be transferred to CBI. @iamRajivBakshi only knows how to harass family members although he has a family of his own. Shame on him.

#transfertoCBI #Justice4Justice #weneedjustice

11:25 PM · Mar 3, 2020 ·Twitter Web App

3791 Retweet **2376** Comment **9129** Likes

Back when Rajiv was a student, English as a subject was petrifying for him. He absolutely hated it and could not write it properly too. In fifth standard, he failed in the English exam. That failure gave him the motivation to master the subject, and since then, he won over his fear. Initially, he used shortcuts to get marks in English paper. He figured out that English grammar exam's template was repetitive. An essay, a letter and a comprehension, followed by some miniscule grammar, which was his adversary. Therefore, he strategized the exam from an early age. He decided to deprioritize the grammar section and focus on the other scoring area. The part about writing a letter would be repetitive too. Either it had to be addressed to the principal, parents, or a relative. Therefore, that was easy to score from. Comprehension was never a problem, as the answers were all there in the question paper itself, and he just needed to find it. Essays would fall in the bucket of role models, hobby, or aspirations of life. One of these three topics would surely be in the question paper. When it came to role models, like all other Indians, Rajiv respected Freedom fighters and took them as role models. Therefore, it was easy to write. Aspirations in life were also not a problem, as he always wanted to be a soldier for the Indian army, and so the essay writing came naturally for this two topics. However, he didn't have a hobby.

Unfortunately, whenever he visited any relatives, the first, second, or third thing they would ask was 'What is your hobby, beta?" Initially, he said he had no hobby, and then everyone would be surprised that how could a kid have no hobby? Therefore, to escape from being judged, he resorted to lie with the most common excuse for a hobby—gardening—although his house did not have a garden or a plantation in a five-kilometer radius. Since then, no one got disappointed when they asked Rajiv about his hobby; so, the lie worked out well for him. Till date, Rajiv did not have a hobby. Although no one asked him those days, but if someone did or some application form had that question, Rajiv would shamelessly lie as 'Gardening'. Rajiv had his own house now, and it had a garden too but never had it ever crossed his mind that he might take up this passion to white some lies that he has been telling for a long time now.

Devika, on the other hand was a passionate woman. Clearly, she had a hobby which she loved to do and most of her time was spent on this hobby of hers. Unfortunately, gossiping as a hobby is not something that you say aloud, so, she also had to fake a hobby. She chose violin playing for this lie. In her early days, she used to say that playing the guitar was her hobby, but most households would have a guitar, and everyone would ask her to play a song on a guitar. Technically, she hadn't strummed the six strings ever, so that hobby did not do well to her. That's when she chose violin as it was a rarer musical instrument. But Karma has been, is, and will always be a bitch. One of her relatives had a violin, and when she was in eleventh standard, she was asked to play the violin in front of a handful of relatives. She ended up creating a music, which can be more appropriately classified as 'noise', and finally, the noise came to a stop when she accidentally tore a string of the violin. Since then, word spread among her relatives that she was pathetic and hopeless in music as a whole.

Considering this background, there was not much that could be expected of Saloni. By heredity and faults of her own, Saloni did not have a hobby either. Around fifth standard, it was Saloni's turn to write an essay about her hobby. Devika was too ashamed to suggest about playing the violin as a hobby, so, the family decided that Saloni should put gardening as her hobby. During Rajiv's school days, the story would end here, but now, the academic curriculum had changed to a more practical, interactive, and visual adaptation. Few days ago, as part of a school exhibition, every student was asked to create a project assignment about their hobby. Saloni and other students had to write down their hobby and submit to the class teacher, so that the class teacher was aware about which student is doing what project. Therefore, it was official. Saloni was doing a project assignment on gardening, without any knowledge of it.

Back at the Bakshi house, it was chaos. The eventuality of the academic project on gardening split the family threefold over the person to be blamed for this. Rajiv and Devika claimed that Saloni should be matured enough to have pen down any other hobbies, such as listening to music or cooking. Saloni and Devika maintained that Rajiv should not have imparted the idea of this hobby to Saloni in the first place. Rajiv alone maintained that Devika and Saloni should have disagreed to his idea of gardening as a hobby. Soon, Rajiv understood that the mother and daughter would force this blame on him. So, he resorted to the one thing he hated, professionally. Bribery. He ordered a 16-inch Double cheese margarita pizza from Dominos. It was their favorite. As usual, the domestic bribery worked, and the crisis was taken up for discussion over some cheesy crusts.

As the discussions began, the problem did not seem that big anymore. The biggest relief was they already had a garden, and the biggest problem was that the garden was empty. Nothing that a few thousand bucks cannot fix. Initially, they thought about taking photographs in someone else's garden but the frequent visit of Saloni's friend charred that idea. Whatever Saloni shows in the exhibition has to be permanent, otherwise, she would be tagged as a falsifier in school. The three of them went together to a nursery to choose plants to fill their garden.

Devika wanted plants which could provide her basic cooking items like chilies, tomatoes, and others. Saloni wanted all the beautiful flowers there were. Rajiv wanted a money plant, only and literally. They brought so many plants that it did not even fit in their Ecosport. The women in the car had to hold a few of them, soiling their beautiful dresses, but none of them cared about it. Once they were home, they spent the next three hours in the garden. They planted each one of them with great care. Rajiv was initially in charge of digging the ground, but soon, Saloni took a keen interest in it and took over from her Dad with a smile. As Rajiv was relieved of his duties, an idea clicked in his mind. He excused himself and left the house.

Within 30 minutes, Rajiv came back. Devika was already pissed off that the ladies were doing all the digging, and she stood up to give Rajiv a piece of her mind. However, as soon as Rajiv opened the rear of the car and brought out the barbeque set, coal and marinated chicken, Saloni and Devika started jumping with joy in the garden. A further 30 minutes on, the barbeque was running in the garden, studio speakers were running loud, cold drinks, and beer chugs, and obviously, the plantation was going on smoothly too. The natural smile and joy in everyone's face and the barbeque added the spice to some great gardening photos. Once the plantation was done, the family stayed back in the garden, relaxing and goggling about the plants they had brought. Saloni brought out some sketch pads, noted down some facts about each of the plants in the garden, and placed those notes beside each of the plants. They felt fantastic to do this together, and it accounted for some of the best family memories. By the time the day was over, they had 17 new family members in the garden. Saloni named all of them and added sticky notes in each of them about their new identities. That night, during dinner, the family decided to formally acknowledge gardening as the hobby for all three of them. Each had a day in the week when they needed to water the plants, and Rajiv was on manure duties.

Saloni's project was a standout in the exhibition. Everyone acknowledged the purity of the pictures and the decoration of the garden and envied the fun the family had, together. She even had a few visitors to their garden, and they even asked multiple questions about the plant, but Saloni could answer them all as she loved reading about them now. Rajiv was not a fan of manure duties, but a happy wife and daughter were reason enough to go through some dirty work. Happy days.

CHAPTER 20

Daring Darling

@daredal

Media sources in @BangalorePolice are saying that the police believes that Mr. Balaram Shetty committed suicide. They are trying to build a false case of depression using the alibis of his daughter's ongoing divorce case and the demise of his wife and daughter in law over the last few years. Sources also say that @PoliceCommissioner is trying to frame this too. We cannot let this Police Gundagiri continue. The Police have not even found the knife by which Mr. Balaram Shetty was stabbed. We have to raise our voice and demand for a fair enquiry, which is only possible if the case is handed over to CBI. I demand CBI for Mr. Shetty.

#IstandforBalaramShetty #shameonBangPolice #CBIMust

#Justice4Justice

8:38 AM · Mar 4, 2020 ·Twitter Web App

7952 Retweet **8634** Comment **13624** Likes

Next morning, as soon as Rajiv arrived at the police station, Mr. Dhole came rushing to him. "Sir, yesterday you were on fire, the whole Kunj Villa went on frenzy."

"I had asked you to monitor each and every house member's behavior after I left. Anything to report on that?"

"Yes, sir. Senapati, one of my constables, reported a secretive fight that broke out between the two brothers, Kuntal and Vicky."

"The youngest against the eldest! What was it about?"

"Senapati could not hear it clearly, as he maintained his distance, but he said that they were pushing each other, and Mr. Kuntal was shouting something along the lines of 'How could you do this to your own family? How could you stoop so low to do this?'"

"Do you think they are talking about the murder?"

Mr. Dhole pretended to think. God knows that he was only pretending. "I am sure it is about the murder, sir."

"Or it can be about the missing cash from the locker. There were four lakh rupees as Mrs. Shetty mentioned. She took two lakh, so there should have been two lakh rupees left, which we do not have a trace of yet."

"Yes, sir, it can be about that too."

"Anything else that your team noted after I left?"

"No, sir, the brothers discussed about our drama and cursed us for an hour or so. We didn't get to hear what they were discussing, but it was intense."

"Ok, another thing, did we inspect the garden of Kunj Villa when we were searching the house? Yesterday, I was gardening and I thought that we may have missed something in the garden; something could have been dug inside. The family members were not allowed to leave the property, so, if anyone had to hide anything outside their room, the garden would be best fit."

"There was nothing unusual in the garden, sir, so we did not check it."

"Check it today; we may be too late already. Check for loose grass. If any of garden area is unearthed to hide something, the grass will be loose. Where ever there is no grass or loose grass, dig that place up."

"Ok, sir but what are we searching for?"

"Anything that should be above ground, and not under it."

"Got it, sir. Our team has been posted there from the day of the murder, and no family member has left the property, so I don't think we will be late. I will inform you about the findings soon."

CHAPTER 21

Arvind Chatterjee

3 h

Media reports confirm that **@Bangalore Police** is shopping vegetables from the market for the Shetty family. They are not allowing any family members to leave the premises, as they do not want media reporters to interview them. What is the police hiding? Why are media not allowed inside the property? The truth must come out. **@Police Commissioner** is declining to comment about this case. We must keep on fighting for Justice.

#UselessBangalorePolice #Justice4Justice

#PoliceCommisionermustresign #RajivBakshimustresign

#Truthwillcomeout

12k Likes 825 Comments 389 Shares

In the afternoon, Rajiv and Mr. Dhole went to Kunj Villa. Rajiv had asked all his officers to be in civil dress in Kunj Villa and instructed them, Sparsh should not know they were police officers. None of the present owners of Kunj Villa left their room to welcome them. Clearly, they were uninvited, but police officers get used to it. Only Hari welcomed them and offered tea. Rajiv politely declined, but by then, Mr. Dhole had already accepted the offer. Rajiv smirked at Mr. Dhole and knocked on Kuntal's room. As soon as Mrs. Aparajita opened the door, Sparsh came running towards Rajiv and hugged him. Rajiv brought out a chocolate from his pocket and gifted to Sparsh, who kissed Rajiv's cheeks and ran away with his gift. Rajiv signaled Aparajita and Kuntal to meet him in the hall.

Kuntal looked tense. “Any news, Inspector?”

“Yes, I would like you to ask Sparsh to play in any other room, as Mr. Dhole will search your room.”

“Again? They have already searched on the first day. Why do you need to search again?”

“Because this time, we know what we are looking for, 2 lakh rupees, cash.”

“What do you mean, Inspector; are you accusing us of stealing the money? And how can you be sure that it's 2 lakhs?”

“Mrs. Pubali Shetty told us that your Dad's locker held 4 lakh rupees, out of which your father gave 2 lakh rupees to her at around 2.00 am. You went to your father's room at 3 am and saw no cash in the locker. So, we need to search your room to confirm that you did not steal that cash.”

“Do we look like thieves to you?” shouted Aparajita.

“It's nothing personal, Mrs. Aparajita; we need to validate from every angle, and this is just routine procedure. No one except your father-in-law and Mr. Kuntal knew about the locker code. Therefore, unless your father gave 2 lakh rupees to someone else between 2 am and 3 am, which is unlikely, those 2 lakh rupees should have been there in the locker when Mr. Kuntal opened it. Therefore, we need to search your room again. I hope you understand and will co-operate.”

Aparajita and an enraged Kuntal hissed like a snake, but they could not strike, so unwillingly agreed and asked Sparsh to go and play in Pubali's room.

Rajiv addressed to Kuntal, “While we wait, do you want to fill me in on another issue please?”

Kuntal reluctantly nodded.

"Yesterday, why did you have a fight with Mr. Vicky?"

Kuntal looked stunned. Aparajita was incensed. She looked towards Kuntal with red fiery eyes and rambled away, leaving the two gentlemen to themselves. Kuntal looked anxious, thinking about the marital perils that lay ahead for him, but he had an imminent threat to deal with presently. He politely responded to the threat. "That's personal, Inspector. I do not want to discuss that."

Any police officer would not stand down, respecting the opponent's privacy. "From what my men heard, it looked like you were accusing your brother of murdering your father. It does not sound private to me."

"No, not at all. We were not discussing about my father's murder," and then he silently added, "It was about a graver sin."

Rajiv knew that with Aparajita away, Kuntal would not be a hard nut to crack. With a stern voice, he said, "So you are not going to tell me about it?"

Kuntal politely declined.

Rajiv took out the handcuffs. "Ok, I am arresting you on suspect of murdering Mr. Balaram and for withholding information."

Kuntal was stunned. "What! Why! How am I a suspect? I told you everything."

"As per information we have, you are the last person to be in your father's room. You may have tried to steal the money, and your father may have caught you stealing; so, you had no other way than to kill him. You have a motive, and so we have reasons to arrest you on suspicion of theft and murder."

"Lies! That is a lie! I told you exactly what happened, I did not steal anything."

"Try explaining that to your family, neighbors, and the judge. I am sure they will believe that you lied to the police initially, but when you were caught lying, you confessed that you tried to steal but found the locker empty."

"Trust me, Inspector, that is exactly what happened, I have told you everything truthfully."

"Then why are you hiding this incident with Mr. Vicky? Tell me the truth about this one, NOW."

"I can't, Inspector, it's about my family's honor. I assure you that it is not about my Dad's murder."

"Ok, then let's go to the police station," Rajiv started to strangle Kuntal into cuffing the handcuffs and said, "If you don't tell the truth, you are coming with me to the police station. I give you my word that if it is not related to your father's murder, I am not telling it to anybody, but I need to hear the truth."

Kuntal was sweating and somehow wriggled out of the grip of Rajiv, or may be, Rajiv let go of it. "Ok, Ok, I will say it, but you must promise me you will not tell it to anyone. It can ruin my family."

Rajiv promised, and, as the saying goes, promises are meant to be broken.

"Vicky Bhaiya doesn't respect any women. He looks at all of them with lust. Many women have complained to my Dad about it, but no one reached out to police due to my Dad's affluence. Around three years back, we had a maid in the house, Rekha. Vicky Bhaiya molested her, and she got pregnant."

Rajiv was flabbergasted. "You mean rape! But there are no records in our books about it! We have records of a molestation case against him, but again, no evidence, so it did not lead to an arrest."

"My Dad always rescued Vicky Bhaiya from arrests, including this time. He made Rekha abort the child and gave five lakh rupees to her. He arranged a job for her in a different city. No one other than him knew which city or where. He punished Vicky Bhaiya by sending him to a mental asylum for six months, that too, off the books. When Bhaiya returned, we thought that he has recovered, but then he started to harass Sabitri Bhabhi."

"What! Mr. Ronit's wife?"

"Yes, he would stare at her for minutes, sit close to her, and find excuses to stay in her room for prolonged time periods when Ronit Bhaiya was not at home. Ronit Bhaiya even had a fight with Vicky Bhaiya on it, and Dad had to step in to stop it. Dad decided to send Vicky Bhaiya again to the same mental asylum, this time for years, but before he could send him away, Sabitri Bhabhi died."

"So, can this bastard, Vicky, have something to do with Mrs. Sabitri's death?"

"It's not that we did not think about it, but there was no evidence, and the plausibility was too wild, so we did not believe that."

"Okay, so what has that to do with your fight with Mr. Vicky?"

"I was fighting for my wife's honor. Since the last fortnight, Vicky Bhaiya has been flirting in the same way with Aparajita, as he did with Sabitri Bhabhi. He keeps frequenting our room, he unnecessarily tries to be close to Aparajita, and, most disgustingly, he inappropriately touched Aparajita the day before yesterday, while he was playing with Sparsh. I found Aparajita crying, and when she told this to me, I could not control my rage. That is why I was fighting him, Inspector. I hope you will understand the sensitivity of this and not tell it to anyone else."

"No I will not but rest assured, I will assure that asshole, Vicky's manliness never gets aroused again, thanks for your time. This problem of yours is my problem now. I will deal with it. It's my promise to you."

"Thank you, Inspector, thanks for understanding."

CHAPTER 22

ArpitaTalukdar

12874 likes

ArpitaTalukdar We request our PM Narendra Modi @PMOIndia to grant CBI enquiry for the murder of Late Justice Balaram Shetty as @BangalorePolice and Rajiv Bakshi has not made any progress in this case after so many days. The @PoliceCommissioner has refrained from giving any statements about the case. What is he hiding? Let's make#Justice4Justice hashtag trend so that our demands can be heard by @PMOIndia

#CBIMust #shameonBangalorePolice #fightforJustice

#Justice4Justice

View all 1674 comments

5 HOURS AGO

Rajiv made some phone calls and waited an hour before knocking on Vicky's door on the first floor. Vicky reluctantly asked Rajiv to take a seat and asked how he could help. Rajiv was livid. Beating about the bush did not suit the temper, so he cut to the chase. "Last time we talked, I asked you to get a good lawyer; did you arrange for one?"

"I haven't done anything wrong, so I don't think I need one."

"Under the Indian Penal Code 378 and various section of IPC 1860, you are going to jail for four years. I think you should reconsider about your lawyer."

"What are you talking about? What do these codes mean? What am I guilty of?"

"You are guilty of misleading a police investigation, and, more importantly, theft of rupees two lakhs from your father's locker on the night of his death. Furthermore, I strongly suspect that you have something to do with your father's murder and I will prove it. When I do, you will rot in jail for your lifetime, and not even your 'good' lawyer can do any damn thing about it, you perverted pig."

"You are lying, Inspector; you don't have any evidence against me, and you are trying to trap me."

"Look who is talking about lying! YOU told me last time that you did not go to your father's room that night. We found your fingerprints on the cigarette that we found in your father's room. Therefore, that's your evidence for misleading the police investigation. We found your fingerprints on your Dad's locker. How about that for evidence about theft?"

Mr. Vicky stumbled two steps back, and he lost the poise he had in his voice but still he muttered, "I did not smoke in Dad's room that night or on any night; you must trust me, Inspector. I don't know how that cigarette bud has my fingerprints; someone is trying to frame me. About the locker, I think I may have touched it some other day when Dad might have asked me to put a paper inside it. I think that is when I left my fingerprints in the locker. What is this story about two lakhs? I did not steal from my Dad."

Rajiv resembled the exact opposite of the wretched figure of Vicky. He mockingly clapped and shouted, "Well played Mr. Vicky, that would have sustained in court well enough in your defense, but I have another piece of evidence against you, which you will find a little hard to counter. Mr. Himanshu Vyas. We arrested him few minutes before, due to illegal possession of two lakh rupees. Guess what? He claims that you gave it to him, early morning, on the day we found that your father had died. He also confessed that you told him that you cannot deposit it in the bank, as all of your family's bank accounts might be searched for this missing money. So, you asked him to keep it for a month, and he would give you 20 thousand from it."

The downcast figure of Mr. Vicky dropped itself to the bed. He looked down on the floor and said, "How did you find him?"

"You should not have called him from your mobile that morning; it leaves a digital trace."

"Unfortunately, I did not know that my Dad would be murdered, and there would be a murder investigation. Are you going to arrest me now?"

"No, not now, but soon. For now, I just want to discuss my theory with you; nothing official, though, as I do not have proof of them, yet."

Vicky did not answer and continued to stare at the floor. Rajiv took a seat and resumed, "You are a pervert who does not even spare his own sister-in-law. You coveted Mrs. Aparajita and frequently visited her room. On one such visit, your brother Kuntal was in the room, so you hid outside and kept gaping at Mrs. Aparajita. That is when Kuntal asked Sparsh about your father's locker code. When Sparsh told about the hint, you over heard it. That is how you knew about the locker code." Vicky did not protest.

"On the night when your father was murdered, once he announced his will, you decided to steal everything in the locker, as he wasn't giving much in inheritance to you. Around 2.30 am, you sneaked into his room." Vicky still did not protest.

"You opened the locker and stole the money. Everything was going according to plan, but sadly, your father woke up and caught you stealing. As he was about to raise the alarm, you could not understand how to save yourself, and though it was not pre-planned, you could not find any other way to stop him and suffocated him to death."

Before Rajiv could proceed, Vicky faced upwards to Rajiv and strongly denied it, "I DID NOT KILL MY FATHER. I went to his room and stole the money and left. I did not smoke in his room. I was dying to get out of the room with the looted money. Why would I smoke in the room? He did not see me steal as he was sleeping. I stole the money and left the room in a hurry. That is exactly what happened. That is the truth."

"I just caught you lying, and you are asking me to believe again that you are telling the truth? I don't care whether you are lying or not. I caught you lying last time, and I will catch you this time too. The truth will be uncovered, along with evidence admissible in court. You are going to rot in jail. For how long, that remains to be seen."

Rajiv turned away from a dejected Mr. Vicky and was about to make his way out of the room, but he stopped. He faced towards Vicky again. "One last thing. If you come close to Mrs. Aparajita or any other lady ever in your life, I already have evidence that you were there in Mr. Balaram's room on the night of the murder. I just need a knife with your fingerprint on it, which is the easiest thing for me to arrange. Whether it is the truth or not, I don't care as long as I am able to keep at least one woman safe in my city. Therefore, you better behave and get that lawyer that we discussed about. Good or bad does not matter. No one can save you now."

Vicky kneeled down and begged Rajiv for forgiveness. He had tears in his eyes, and he repeatedly yelled about being innocent, but all his cries fell on deaf ears as Rajiv left the room spitefully.

CHAPTER 23

India 4Life

@india4life

This case has to be transferred to the CBI now as the @BangalorePolice have not cracked any of it yet. @PMOIndia must step in and act fast before all the evidences are corrupted or erased.

#transfertoCBI #Justice4Justice #BangalorePolicesucks

#RajivBakshiloser

10:32 PM · Mar 4, 2020 ·Twitter Web App

13678 Retweet **5689** Comment **20145** Likes

Back at his home, Rajiv looked exhausted. He was tired of thinking. It hadn't not even been a week since the murder of Mr. Balaram, and already the Police Commissioner was calling him twice daily to put someone behind bars, be it anyone, innocent or guilty. Rajiv could not blame him. He knew well that the murder of former Chief Justice Balaram Shetty was the Breaking News clincher in media. The #Justice4Justice hashtag had gone viral on Twitter, and everyone was using it to voice his or her opinion about the inefficiency of the police force in solving the case.

Rajiv said to himself, “They think that the murderer roams about, shouting that he killed someone. They don't have the faintest idea about the hitches we go through to round up the killer. Unfortunately, our Police Commissioner thinks likewise.”

There were protests around the city and candle marches, all demanding for the murderer to be apprehended and punished. Slogans were raised for passing the case to CBI as the Bangalore police was inefficient. Experience has taught Rajiv to ignore the digital buzz and chasers from higher management. Murder cases need to follow a certain pace and time, and if that is not provided, chances are that the derivative clues can be missed. Therefore, Rajiv switched himself off from all the official and family duties and locked himself in his bedroom. Saloni and Devika were used to this solitary confinement phase of Rajiv's investigation and gave Rajiv the space he needed.

Rajiv kept on thinking about all the information he had gathered and tried to piece them all together, but most of the pieces of puzzle were still missing. He had sorted out the theft of the money, but the case in hand was for homicide, not burglary. He had to solve who killed Mr. Balaram Shetty, but he did not make much head way in that. He had his doubts on many, but more the number of suspects, more were the chances that he was wrong. He wanted to believe that Vicky had cold bloodedly killed his father, but something did not feel right about it, and most importantly, the locked doors of Mr. Balaram Shetty's bedroom nullified all theories. As the door was locked from the inside, the murderer had no other way out, than to escape through the open ventilator shaft in the bathroom. No one in the household except Kuntal had the physicality to do so, and even then, the murderer had to be immensely athletic to climb down unharmed. However, years of family life had rendered Kuntal lethargic and unfit for such a task. Even the whisky was not helping to string new theories together, so he called Mr. Dhole and asked him to visit his home.

“Mr. Dhole, I am not making any progress in the case. We are not even close to finding the murderer. We have to do something, fast. The netizens are pulling the strings on this case over twitter, and we have orders to arrest someone immediately, be it innocent or guilty. I want to ensure that we arrest the latter, so I called to discuss our findings.”

Mr. Dhole had never seen Rajiv, so much dejected. Rajiv looked like he was losing his self-belief. Instead of answering to Rajiv, Mr. Dhole picked up his desk phone, called someone, and shouted at him for two minutes. After disconnecting that call, he answered to Rajiv, "How can you solve the case without the autopsy report, sir. I am sure the autopsy report will clear everything for us. I have arranged for it to be delivered to my home by 10 pm. You don't have to wait till tomorrow for it."

Rajiv smiled and thanked Mr. Dhole.

Mr. Dhole resumed, "Apologies for asking, sir, but something keeps bothering me about this case. Do you really think anyone in Mr. Shetty's family is fit or slim enough to climb to the open shaft in Mr. Balaram's washroom and come down by the pipes? Even our police officers could not do it."

"I keep thinking about it too; the chances are slim, but human brain can give us power to do strange things in desperate times. It can even help you walk over burning coal without feeling any pain. I know the chances are slim, but let's not rule it out."

"But how can the killer be in a desperate situation, sir? The killer will always have the easier route open, which is going out through the main door of Mr. Balaram's room. Why would he have to go out the ventilator shaft? It does not make any sense."

"To make it look like the killer was an outsider. If the doors were unlocked, the obvious suspicion would go to all the family members. However, as the doors were locked from the inside, it would be difficult to prove in court that it was an inside job. As you said, none of the family members look like they can make that climb and go out of that small hole and then down the pipes. That is going to be their defense strategy if this goes to the court."

"So, what do we do, sir?"

Rajiv sulked, "We do what we can do. We investigate, find the killer, and present our findings to the court. After that, it's for the lawyers to dwell and drag the case for years to come."

"Let's not be negative, sir; maybe the autopsy report will help us in getting justice for the former Justice." Mr. Dhole smirked for playing with words. After half an hour, Mr. Dhole left for his home and assured Rajiv that he would send the autopsy report as soon as he received it.

Around 11 pm, Mr. Dhole called Rajiv excitedly, "Sir, the post mortem report is here, and it is fascinating. It puts to rest all our existing theories. I have Whatsapp it to you, please have a read."

It was the most exciting news Rajiv had heard the whole day. After reading it through, Rajiv called Mr. Dhole. "How can this be! Why did not we see anything like it in Mr. Balaram's room?"

"I don't know, sir; I am not able to make head or tail of it."

"Ok, meet me at Kunj Villa first thing tomorrow morning; there are many a things that we need to check."

CHAPTER 24

@daredal

#Justice4Justice is 13th on Trending hashtags. We need to make it the most trending hashtag, so share it more. Our protests need to reach @PMOIndia so that the case is transferred to CBI urgently.

#IstandforBalaramShetty #PMOtrasfercasetoCBI #CBIMust

#Justice4Justice

10:27 AM · Mar 5, 2020 · Twitter Web App

8124 Retweet **4782** Comment **15432** Likes

Mr. Dhole and Rajiv carried on a day-long investigation at the Kunj Villa but in the evening, Rajiv had to leave early, as it was his day to pick up Saloni from her tuition classes. Rajiv and his wife both were working parents. They had the parental duties divided among themselves. Every Tuesday, Thursday, and Sunday, Rajiv would be responsible for preparing breakfast and tiffin for the family. Rajiv would drop Saloni to school on Tuesday and Thursdays. On Sunday, Rajiv would cook lunch and dinner for the family too. This gave some space in Mrs. Bakshi's private life; she at least had one day in a week when she could relax. Every weekday, Saloni had at least one private tuition after school. Today, it was Rajiv's duty to pick his daughter up from the tuition centre.

In Kunj Villa, there were few points which needed further investigation. Rajiv had no other choice than to leave instructions for Mr. Dhole and hope that Mr. Dhole would follow it correctly.

Rajiv had to pick up Saloni nearby to a temple, which was near the tuition centre. There was traffic near the temple; so, Rajiv parked a few cars away from the pickup spot. He kept a lookout for his daughter.

Being the only child of the Bakshis', Saloni was always pampered and brought up like the princess of the house. Not that it is bad, but having a princess in your castle comes with consequences. Saloni was moody and bossy by nature, and she herself had taken the liberty of crowning herself the Queen of the house. The whole police department as well as criminals in Bangalore was afraid of the Superintendent of Police, Mr. Rajiv Bakshi, but if Rajiv was afraid of someone, it was not his wife, but his loving daughter, Saloni. Saloni had just stepped into that age bracket where every child becomes the parent of their parent. So, if Rajiv did anything wrong, Saloni would immediately blame it on Rajiv's age and the associated downfalls of getting old. Rajiv hated to hear about it but he did not have any words to protest. After all, anything he said might hurt his Princess. So, he would patiently be an audience to the 'getting old' speech.

If the Princess could not find her Dad's car and had to wait in the road for five minutes, Rajiv could foresee her daughter's parenting lectures. Therefore, he stepped out of his car to be on the lookout for Saloni, so that he could wave to her as soon as he caught sight of her.

It wasn't long before he saw Saloni along the aisle of the road, but there was someone else with her. The boy walking along with Saloni looked to be from her class. He had spiked hair and wore a headband and thick beads on his right hand. Rajiv remembered the days when he used to go to tuitions, 35 years back. Stripped shirt, untucked, and cotton full pants. His parents only allowed him to wear jeans if it was someone's birthday. His mother would oil his hair before he left home, and it would be combed to lie down horizontally. His mother told him that one should look like a nerd while going to tuitions, as that is a place of worship, and Rajiv was going to learn something new. That is how Rajiv would be showing respect to the teacher. Rajiv shifted back to reality. The boy walking beside Saloni was the polar opposite of how Rajiv was 35 years ago. Rajiv thought about walking forwards to greet his princess, but suddenly, the boy held Saloni's hands. Saloni stopped and looked at their hands held together. She looked up at the boy and blushed. Rajiv felt an eerie sensation that he had never felt before. Rajiv did not know yet what was it, but it was a new feeling. As Saloni and the boy walked closer to the temple, the boy started getting cozy. He wrapped his arms around Saloni's shoulders. Saloni did not protest. Rajiv had already pulled out his gun and pointed it at the boy, in his thoughts. In reality, he hid himself behind a tree. He wanted to see where this was leading.

Saloni and the boy were walking holding hands, giggling and blushing, looking at each other. As they reached the temple, Saloni asked the boy to lend his ears. The boy happily obeyed. Saloni whispered something in his ears, the boy reacted to be shocked at what his daughter had to say and soon, both of them started blushing and smiling awkwardly. Rajiv had enough. He was about to step out of his hiding and go over to Saloni, but suddenly, Saloni turned around. She was apparently searching for Rajiv's car. A strange impulsion barred Rajiv to show himself to his daughter. He continued to hide behind the tree, knowing well that he was welcoming the 'getting old' speech from his daughter. Saloni turned back towards the boy and said something to him. The boy looked around to check if anyone was looking at them and within a flash of a second, kissed Saloni on the lips.

Rajiv felt like he was having a heart attack. His rage knew no bounds. He got out of his hiding and rushed towards Saloni. Rajiv knew that Saloni was strong and independent, and she did not need him to defend herself, but his fatherly instinct would not listen to logic at that time. Saloni looked stunned at being kissed suddenly, that too in a public place. She surely wasn't prepared for it. She looked at the boy furiously and gave him a tight slap. Rajiv was running now and a few meters away, but even he could hear the sound of the slap. The boy got embarrassed at being slapped in front of everyone. Every passersby were looking at him.

He looked in disbelief at Saloni. He covered his left cheek with his left hand. Suddenly, the boy swore at Saloni and raised his right hand to slap Saloni. Saloni ducked by instinct, but before the boy could slap his precious daughter, Rajiv shouted at the boy, "DON'T YOU DARE TOUCH MY GIRL, YOU PIECE OF SHIT!" The boy looked at the raged eyes of Rajiv, running towards him. The boy got scared and made a run for it, into the darkness. Rajiv wanted to follow the boy, but Saloni looked at her Dad and hugged him tight. She was crying. Rajiv was distraught. He had never seen his princess cry like this. He felt like going after the boy and teaching him a lesson, but his princess held him tight. He caressed her hair and said,"I saw what happened, beta; you were brave. I am so proud of you. Nothing happened, beta, don't cry please. Aren't you my strong princess?"

Saloni didn't look up but continued to sob, tucking her head in Rajiv's chest. "Please promise me, Daddy, that you will not tell about this to Mom."

"I will not tell this to your Mom, dear. I promise. Who was that bastard?"

"Dhruv Seth. He is my class mate." Saloni stopped sobbing and looked up to her Dad. A sense of fear flickered through her young eyes. "Dad, he proposed to me 2 weeks back. I liked him, but I did not say anything to him. As I did not answer, he assumed that he is my boyfriend. I did not tell it to you or Mom, as nothing was official. I would have surely told you everything, if it were official."

Rajiv gestured to his daughter that it isn't a problem. After the reassurance, Saloni resumed, "He always found excuses to spend time with me. I found him waiting for me outside the tuitions today. He told me that he wanted to walk with me to the temple. He suddenly held my hands today. I did not say anything for that, but I do not know what took over him that he suddenly kissed me!"

Saloni started crying again and said, "I never meant to kiss him, but he is a rough boy. He is infamous for being notorious and a bully. He will not like that I slapped him. He will surely hurt me at the class. He will not be quite about it. He has wicked friends too, and I am sure they are going to hurt me, Dad. What do I do now?"

"You are MY daughter, dear. There is NO ONE in the whole of India who can harm you. I assure you that he will not even come close to you. Come, beta, let's go home. Nothing happened. You did the right thing. Daddy will take care of the rest. I promise. That prick will not bother you again."

Saloni looked up, and she was still sobbing. "Are you telling the truth Dad?"

Rajiv kissed her daughter's forehead, assured her, and asked her to walk towards the car, which was parked a few meters away.

Back home, Rajiv did not tell anything to Devika, just as he had promised her daughter. However, he was restless and disgusted. Devika assumed there might be some problem with the ongoing investigation and gave Rajiv the space he needed.

Rajiv was in the board of trustees in Saloni's school. He had helped the Principal of the school multiple times with police matters, regarding parent's complaint or a teacher whacking a student. Each time, the Principal assured him, if there was anything he could help Rajiv with, he would be just a call away. It was time for Rajiv to make that call. Rajiv called the Principal and explained the situation to him. Rajiv then discussed about the favor he needed from the Principal. He got the number of Dhruv's parents from the Principal and gave them a call. He told them about the whole incident and threatened to lodge a formal police complaint against Dhruv for sexual abuse of his daughter. Dhruv's parents begged Rajiv to reconsider and pledged that they would do everything in their power to punish Dhruv and ensure that this never happened again.

Rajiv considered their advice and said, "My daughter is worried about how she can be in the same class with Dhruv after this incident. I have the same concern too. I understand your concern that a police complain would ruin Dhruv's life, but I cannot afford to take no actions about it. Specially, I cannot let Dhruv be in the same school with my Daughter. The best I can do is that I will not lodge any formal police complaint, but your son will be rusticated from school, and you will have to find another school for him."

Dhruv's parents begged Rajiv to reconsider, as this was the middle of the session, and this would mean that Dhruv would lose an academic year between 10th and 12th standard, which will reflect in his CV too. However, Rajiv was not ready to allow Dhruv to be in the same school, as Saloni and he would not step down from this punishment. It was either this or the police complaint. Dhruv's parents had little choice but to accept this.

Rajiv called the Principal and told him about his conversation with Dhruv's parents. The Principal thanked him for not raising a police complaint about it, which would be negative for the school's image. Within the same night, the Principal issued a rustication order for Dhruv Seth and had it delivered to Dhruv's parents. When all was done, around 11 pm, Rajiv went to Saloni's room and assured her that Dhruv would never trouble her again. The Princess hugged the King.

CHAPTER 25

Arvind Chatterjee

3 h

Finally, **@Bangalore Police** has arranged for a press meeting tonight to discuss the progress of Late Honorable Justice Balaram Shetty's murder investigation. Hope they have some important updates.

#Justice4Justice #Truthwillcomeout

9k Likes 489 Comments 178 Shares

Next morning, Rajiv went to Kunj Villa again, but this time, he was not alone. There were around half a dozen other police officers with him. Word spread fast around Kunj Villa, and this time, everyone stepped out of their room and came down to the drawing room out of curiosity. Rajiv welcomed all of them and told that he has news for them and he wanted to discuss a few findings with the siblings. Every one enquired the same thing, "Did you find out who killed our father?"

"Patience, everyone, let's not draw conclusions here. We shall discuss our findings and then take it from there."

No one bought it. Mr. Ronit said, "So, who is the killer? Where is he? Did you catch him?"

"No, Mr. Ronit, we are working on it, but please take a seat, as I have a few things to discuss which might interest you."

Everyone took a seat except the police officers. Hari stood by the kitchen so that he could hear everything.

Rajiv brought out a piece of paper from his pockets and resumed, “This is a copy of the autopsy report of Mr. Balaram Shetty. As per the report, the primary reason of death is,” he gave a theatrical pause and then, “Choking! Mr. Shetty died due to insufficient air flow to his lungs!”

Whispers went all around the room, and everyone looked surprised. “But we saw the stab wounds, and we saw blood!” “Who could have done this to our dear Dad!”“When did that bastard suffocate my Dad? What is the exact time of death?”

Rajiv said, “The official report says that the time of death is between 1.30 to 2.30 am. However, we believe we have the exact time of death. It is around 2.30 am.”

Aparajita spoke up, “How can you be so sure officer?”

“There were no marks of choking around Mr. Balaram's neck, so he must have been suffocated with something soft, like a pillow, which will not leave a mark. We had run a fingerprint check on Mr. Balaram's pillow, and we can confirm that he was suffocated using his own pillow.”

“How can you be sure of it? Did you find any fingerprint match from the pillow? Do you know who suffocated our Dad?” asked Pubali.

Rajiv replied, “Let's start from the beginning, shall we?”

Rajiv walked towards Kuntal and said, “Mr. Kuntal was looking to move out of Kunj Villa, to a more spacious house or flat, where he could leave happily with his family. He had to ask for financial help from Mr. Balaram Shetty, as he could not afford to buy a flat without financial aid from his father. However, he knew that Mr. Shetty would not entertain the idea of his youngest son moving out of Kunj Villa. He also knew that he had a fair reason for moving out, as his room in Kunj Villa was not palatial, considering three family members were living in it. That along with the emotional backdrop around Sparsh's future would surely provide Mr. Kuntal with an opportunity to churn out some financial aid from his father. However, it could be done only once, as Mr. Shetty was not an easy person to fool."

All this while, Rajiv was circling around Kuntal, like a vulture. He ended his sentence with a question, "Am I right so far, Mr. Kuntal?"

Kuntal's silence and shameful eyes gave away the unspoken truth.

Rajiv continued, "No one in Kunj Villa knew how much cash was inside the aristocrat safe in Mr. Balaram Shetty's room, but everyone assumed 7 figure sums. Kuntal had just one chance to ask for financial help, but he did not have a figure he could ask for. He knew that he could get as much as was available in the safe. Therefore, he needed to unlock the safe and check how much riches it held. As Mr. Balaram Shetty would not tell anyone the pass code for the safe, Mr. Kuntal thought of using his secret weapon. He manipulated his own son, Sparsh, to ask Mr. Balaram Shetty about the pass code for the locker. Coming from his grandson, it would not create any suspicion. However, when Sparsh asked it to his granddad, Mr. Balaram Shetty only gave a hint of the code of the locker to our dear Sparsh. Mr. Kuntal figured out the code successfully from the hint. The moment Mr. Balaram Shetty declared his will, Mr. Kuntal realized that he needed to ask his father for the money to buy a new flat urgently. That night, he went to Mr. Balaram Shetty's room at 3 am, hoping his father would be asleep by then. He opened the safe using the pass code to check how much cash it had, but unfortunately, found it to be empty. All of this, Mr. Kuntal has already confessed."

Rajiv paused, but no one interrupted; instead, everyone looked at Kuntal with condemning eyes. He walked towards Vicky and said, "When Sparsh told the hint to his parents, Mr. Vicky overheard it. Mr. Vicky used to frequent Kuntal's room due to a personal matter but this time, he was at the right place at the right time. Just when Mr. Kuntal asked Sparsh about the hint, Mr. Vicky overheard it. It was easy to make out the code from the hint, which he did. On the night of the murder, Mr. Balaram Shetty had declared his will, and none of the siblings were happy with it as a major part of the inheritance was being donated. Mr. Vicky was enraged too, and he thought about stealing the money from the safe in his Dad's room. Therefore, around 2.30 am, Mr. Vicky went to Mr. Balaram's room to steal the money left in the locker. As he was stealing the 2 lakh rupees left in the safe, Mr. Balaram must have woken up and caught him stealing. Mr. Balaram was about to raise the alarm and wake everyone up. In that desperate moment, Mr. Vicky must have found no other way to silence Mr. Balaram, got hold of the pillow, and suffocated his father to death."

Vicky erupted, "What the fuck are you talking about, Inspector? I told you a hundred times that I did not kill my father. Why would I kill my father? Yes, I confess that I stole money from the locker, and I took the cheque of 60 lakhs from the locker and tore it apart, but I did not kill him, I would never kill him. I loved him. You cannot put it on me, just because you do not have anyone else to put it on."

Mr. Vicky's siblings supported his defense with a protesting hum.

Rajiv shouted back, "Then how do you explain your fingerprints on Mr. Balaram's pillow? Yesterday, after receiving the forensic report, we ran fingerprints check over Mr. Balaram's pillow and we found your fingerprints all over it. You have yourself said that you did not go to your father's room in the last 3 days before your father died. Hari has confirmed that the pillow covers were washed two days before the murder. So, how can it have your fingerprints?"

"I don't know. I may have touched it that night."

Rajiv mockingly replied, "While stealing the money! How? Suddenly, you had some compassion and love for your father while stealing his money, and you caressed his face and may have touched the pillow? You think we are stupid? Even if you did so, how can you have your fingerprints in the lower side of the pillow, which is towards the bed and not towards the head? How can you have your fingerprints there?"

All other family members were shocked at this sudden rise of the tempo, but none came forward to defend their brother.

Mr. Vicky's voice lowered down, but he still protested, “But I did not do it, Inspector; you must trust me. I did not kill my father.”

“Then how would you explain the cigarette bud we found in your father's room, the same brand that you smoke and with your fingerprints in it? Will you still say that you did not smoke it? Does it make any sense that you smoke it inside your father's room after stealing his money, while he is alive and sleeping? Why would you do that?”

“I know it sounds like I did it, Inspector, but you must trust me, I did not do it.”

“That is something you must explain to the court; presently, I am arresting you on charges of murder of Mr. Balaram Shetty.” Rajiv looked back and signaled one of the police officers to arrest Mr. Vicky and take him away. While the officer carried out the order, few family members tried to protest but could not find any words to convey the protest and stayed silent. Vicky continuously shouted that he was innocent and that he did not kill his father.

When the police took Vicky away, the other members looked at Rajiv in awe, and then they looked at each other but did not say anything. Rajiv broke the awkward silence. “You know another interesting thing that came out from the autopsy report?”

CHAPTER 26

ArpitaTalukdar

♡ ▢ ∇ ⊓

5722 likes

ArpitaTalukdar As per sources, @BangalorePolice is trying to frame family members of Late Honorable Justice Balaram Shetty for his murder. I think they are just wiping their hands off the complexity of catching the actual murderer as he must have fled and covered his tracks by now. We must not let it happen. We must protest against it. Do you agree?

#catchactualkiller #shameonBangalorePolice

#sparefamilymembers #Justice4Justice

View all 341 comments

15 MINUTES AGO

Everyone thought that the nightmare was over, but soon figured out it had just begun.

"There was an excess amount of Zolpidem in Mr. Balaram's blood. This chemical is used in sleeping pills. Looks like before he was suffocated to death, he had taken a few too many sleeping pills too, sufficient to kill him in his sleep. So, if Mr. Vicky had not suffocated him, Mr. Balaram Shetty would still be dead by morning."

For the first time during this investigation, Hari spoke up without being asked to speak, "But Saab never took sleeping pills. He always said that it was a slow poison. That is why he never drank alcohol or smoked cigarettes, as he believed that it is cheating on your own soul! Why would he take so many sleeping pills?"

Rajiv looked at Hari and nodded at him. "I know how well you know your former master, and it is a fair question. Why would he take it? May be he did not take it. Someone slipped it in his drink or food!" Rajiv turned to Pubali. "Mrs. Pubali, you had confessed that you gave a sleeping pill to your father, didn't you?"

Mrs. Pubali staggered at this sudden jolt of attention to herself. The whole room turned their gaze towards her. "I only gave him one pill, Inspector, because he wanted it from me. I only gave one." Her voice trembled.

"Did you also hand him over the glass of water to take the pill?"

Pubali took a second before she answered in the affirmative.

Rajiv stepped a few steps closer to Pubali, whose cosmetics were giving way to sweat. "How many sleeping pills do you take per day?"

"Normally, I take one, but sometimes, I take two."

"We did a small inspection of your prescribed sleeping pill yesterday. It contains Zolpidem, and it dissolves in water. Then we looked at your medical history. You had bought a new bottle of pills from Medplus on 24th February, which is about 5 days before the murder. This bottle consists of 60 pills, so if you take even two a day, you should have around 40 pills as of yesterday. But we found only 30 pills left, and definitely you did not take 2 pills each day. So, we have no other option than to believe that you dissolved around 14 pills in the glass of water you gave to your father, along with that single pill."

Pubali sprung like a cat. "What! Are you mad, you asshole? Why the fuck would I kill my father? I don't know where my pills have gone, but who gave you the right to search my room without my permission?"

Rajiv dived into his pockets, fetched a piece of paper, and flashed it. "This is the search warrant, without this I could not produce this evidence in court anyway. Also, I have a witness and a video recording of the count of pills you have left."

"I will screw you for this, Inspector. How dare you accuse me of such horrendous crime? I loved my father, and I had no reason to kill him."

Rajiv was still composed. "Yes, I thought about it too. Why would you kill your father? Of course, the cheque of 60 lakhs to charity is a motive. Killing your Dad would be one way to stop that money from going to charity, but it did not fit well. Then I met your lawyer, who is fighting your divorce case. His pending fees had mounted to 3.5 lakhs, and if you didn't pay him urgently, he threatened that he will intentionally lose the case, and you will get no alimony. He also mentioned to me that your father, Mr. Balaram Shetty, was against this divorce and preferred your husband instead of you. Your father even gave your husband's lawyer legal advice about your divorce case. Therefore, now, you have a definite reason to be angry and a motive. Your father had announced his will, and if he died, you would get the money you need to pay to your lawyer. In addition, you knew and hated the fact that your Dad was helping your husband's lawyer and not his own daughter. Isn't that true?"

Pubali subdued her tone; she could not act brave any more. Her defense systems were breached. She sulked and took her seat on the sofa. "Yes, that is true, and I hated my father for it. How can he think that his own daughter is wrong and his son in law is right? He does not even know his son-in-law for 6 months, and still he took his side. However, I did not murder him, and I did not give him the sleeping pills. I only gave him one; trust me, Inspector. I don't know what happened to the other pills. I don't count them every day."

"I want to trust you, Mrs. Pubali. However, the forensic report of the glass in which you dissolved your single sleeping pill and gave to your father persuades me to believe in medical facts. The report says that the volume of residual traces of Zolpidem found on the glass cannot be from a single sleeping pill but a minimum of 10 to 15 sleeping pills. Therefore, evidence compels me to doubt your words. I have enough reasons to arrest you, and you can give your defense to the court. As of now, I am arresting you on charges of poisoning your father, Mr. Balaram Shetty."

During her arrest, Mrs. Pubali did not resist much. She did not even look up, not even once, at her siblings. The family watched in silence till she had crossed the horizon of the door and was no longer in view.

Kuntal spoke up after a minute of silence. "My brother and my sister? Both of them killed my father! How could they?"

"Same way you wanted to steal your father's money but couldn't as it was already stolen."

"Stealing is different, Inspector, but does it mean that, when I went to my Dad's room, he was already dead?"

"Yes, he was dead by then."

"But in the morning, we saw blood and stab marks, how did that happen? I definitely did not see any blood when I went to his room at 3 am, that night."

Rajiv tapped on Kuntal's arms and said, "Good question Mr. Kuntal. About that one, we had a hard time identifying the weapon which inflicted the stab wounds. We could not find it anywhere in Mr. Balaram's room or the house. We searched for it everywhere, but without the weapon, we were not able to finalize what happened around that. Finally, we found it in your lawn, buried underneath the grass. The trick was to find the grass or soil which was loose, which must have been dug up few days ago."

Rajiv turned towards Mr. Dhole and signaled him to bring the knife with which Mr. Balaram was stabbed.

CHAPTER 27

@daredal

BREAKING NEWS @BangalorePolice arrests two siblings of Late Justice Balaram Shetty on murder charges. Why would any son or daughter kill such a respected and honest father? I smell something fishy here. I think they are trying to wind up the case somehow so that it does not go to CBI.

#Innocentsarrested #CBIMust #Justice4Justice

11:53 AM · Mar 6, 2020 · Twitter Web App

5118 Retweet **2341** Comment **7821** Likes

Kuntal sounded curious. "Why did anyone stab him when he was already dead? Also, how can you be sure that this knife was used to stab him?"

Rajiv turned towards Kuntal. "I think that the person who stabbed your father did not know that he was already dead. Therefore, he stabbed him to kill. It cannot be a coincidence that this person stabbed your father on the night that he declared his will. Therefore, I would say the benefactors of the will would have something to do with it. We have got Mr. Balaram Shetty's blood stains from this knife, which confirms that he was stabbed with it."

"Why can't it be someone from outside? Dad had quite a few

enemies. He had punished many criminals, so one of them could have done it."

"Yes, that is a possibility, but the fingerprints on this knife rules out that possibility."

"Whose fingerprints did you find in it?"

"Before I answer that, I would like to apprise you that we found another blood stain in this knife. It was faded, but our lab experts did a commendable job to get the DNA extract out of it. This DNA extract did not match with anyone from the family, so we dug through some old records and finally found a match. This blood stain matched to the late Mrs. Sabitri Shetty."

Ronit leaped up from the sofa. "You mean to say that Sabitri used this knife to commit suicide?"

"I would not term it as suicide anymore; rather, I can confirm that it was a murder. As you all know, a kitchen knife was found by the body, during the initial investigation of Mrs. Sabitri Shetty's suicide, but looks like it was just a decoy to cover up the murder and stage it like a suicide."

"But who? Who murdered my wife, and how can you be so sure of it?"

"Because we found your fingerprints on it, Mr. Ronit. If your wife committed suicide, your fingerprints should not be there on the knife she was stabbed with. I think you made a mistake; you should have used a different knife to kill your father, and now, I will charge you with two murders, that of Mr. Balaram and Mrs. Sabitri."

"What are you talking, Inspector? Why would I kill Sabitri or Dad! I did not kill them. I was not even in my senses the night Dad died. After Dad announced his will, I got so upset that I came back to my room and took a whole drag of marijuana. I passed out immediately and woke up in the morning. I did not know anything of it Inspector, trust me, please."

Rajiv pitched his voice a bit louder this time. "The morning your father was found dead, the police force had guarded the house and did not allow anyone to go out of the complex. However, the guards informed me that before the rooms were searched, you went out to the gardens for a smoke. That is exactly when you buried it in the garden, Mr. Ronit, so that it could not be recovered during the search of your room. After Mrs. Sabitri's death, you wanted to marry your office colleague, with whom you are still having an affair. You even told your father about it, but he was strictly against it, and he would not let you remarry. If he had lived and his cheque of 60 lakhs would have been cashed out to the charity, your future plans would have been screwed. That's why you killed him. Isn't that right, Mr. Ronit?"

Mr. Ronit looked messed up and in two minds. He looked up to answer but decided to stay put. He looked at Kuntal and Aparajita with pleading eyes, but when his eyes met Rajiv, he stringently said, "I will not try to defend myself in front of you. I will only speak in front of my lawyer. You will have to explain to the court about your accusations. Most importantly, how will you explain to the court about the locked door? My father's room was locked from the inside. If I stabbed my father, how did I get out? You don't expect the judge to believe that I would fit in that small hole in the washroom, do you?"

"Oh, that was a master stroke, I must say. I lost many a night's sleep, figuring this one out. Everything fell into place, but I just could not figure out how you managed to get out of the room, when the doors were locked from the inside. Yes, I do not believe you would fit in that ventilation hole. Therefore, I revisited all the photos of Mr. Balaram's room, which were taken during our investigation. Do you know what I found? The room was never locked from the inside."

Kuntal spoke up in shock. "What are you saying Inspector? The room was locked from the inside; we had to use brute force to break it open? I can confirm that on behalf of my brother."

"I agree you had to use brute force to open it, but I disagree that you had to 'break it' open. I will show you; let's go upstairs to Mr. Balaram Shetty's room."

Everyone went up the stairs and into Mr. Balaram's room. As everyone went in, Rajiv closed the door and locked it using the padlock at the top of the door. "This padlock still works fine. This is the only lock in the door. On the night of the murder, let's assume that this lock was used to lock the door from inside. Therefore, when you broke the door open, from outside, this lock should have been broken or a piece of wood would have broken off from the door frame, which would have actually opened the door. Do you see any sign of damage to the locks or the frame?"

Everyone looked carefully at the lock in the door and the doorframe and answered in negative.

Kuntal questioned, "Then how was the door locked? As I said, I am sure it was locked. We had to kick it open and it did not budge till the 3 of us kicked simultaneously."

"Yes, of course it looked like it was locked, I know. Mr. Kuntal, please go ahead and touch the two door hinges that attach the doors to the wooden door frame."

Kuntal was surprised at the request but obliged. He inspected the door hinges of the left door panel and upon inspection, he said, "There is something sticky here; what is it?"

"It is industrial glue, used to bond metals together. It's transparent too, so we could not figure it out previously. After stabbing his father while leaving the room, Mr. Ronit must have pasted this industrial glue all over the door hinges, on both the door panels. He then moved out of the room and closed the door from the outside, without locking it. This glue would take some seconds to set in, and once it had set firmly, it would not allow the door hinge to move anymore, thus not allowing the door to open. Whenever you open any doors by any angle, say 90 degrees, it's the door hinges that actually move by that 90 degrees, allowing the door to open. In this case, as the door hinges are glued and cannot move, the door looks to be locked. As there are no locks outside and the door won't budge open, all of you assumed that the door was locked from the inside. So, when you kicked the door open, you did not break any locks, you only broke the bond of the glue in the door hinges."

Everyone looked in awe at Rajiv and then at Ronit. Mr. Dhole arrested Ronit and took him away to the police station.

Kuntal and Aparajita took some time to settle on the fact that all their brothers had killed Mr. Balaram Shetty in their own ways. They were living in a family of murderers. Thinking of their child's safety, they thanked Rajiv multiple times, whereas Hari prepared chai and pakodas for all the police officers.

CHAPTER 28

@india4life

The evidence provided by @iamRajivBakshi cannot be denied. It is clear enough that @BangalorePolice have caught the guilty. Great work @iamRajivBakshi and I fell in love with you again. You never cease to surprise us. Love you @iamRajivBakshi and a huge thanks to @BangalorePolice to serve the due justice,

#Justiceserved #Justice4Justice #BangalorePoliceisthebest

#RajivBakshihatsoff

9:46 PM · Mar 6, 2020 ·Twitter Web App

16843 Retweet **15634** Comment **22196** Likes

Rajiv hosted a press conference, confirmed his findings about the murder of Mr. Balaram Shetty, and highlighted all the evidence. Soon, the netizens went crazy over Rajiv. Yet again, Rajiv Bakshi had pulled out a masterpiece. After the Green Man serial killer case, Rajiv was already the face of faith for the police force. He was the hero of the city, and yet again, he proved his merit. Everyone was lauding him for bringing some spoiled brats to justice, who could even murder their own father for materialistic benefits. The case about Mr. Balaram Shetty's murder shook the core believes of any India family. No one could come to terms with the idea that someone's own sons and daughter could murder their father, that too all three at once, on the same night. Everyone roared and cheered for Bangalore police and demanded tough sentences for the murderers. They demanded that justice be served quickly for the death of a glorified Chief Justice, who dedicated his life to serve justice to the corrupt.

Rajiv was getting congratulation calls from all around. The

Commissioner went as far as discussing Rajiv's promotion, but Rajiv knew that the Commissioner would soon forget that he ever said it.The reporters gathered outside the police station and were barking for a quote from Rajiv, but Rajiv was as camera shy as it gets. He sent others to provide statements to media, but the media kept insisting for him. They only wanted him as the face of Bangalore Police force. Finally, Rajiv had to come out of the station to give the statement but was amazed to see the crowd that had gathered to cheer him. Thousands of youths were raising slogans and cheering him on. He was moved by it and thanked all of them for coming to support him. Few young girls came forward from the crowd as their representatives with a huge garland for him. To his utter surprise, Saloni was among those girls, with the biggest and proudest smile on her face. Rajiv thanked all of them, waved at everyone in the crowd, and turned towards the police station to go back in. However, the reporters stopped him and handed him a microphone to address to the crowd that had gathered. Rajiv was not much of a speaker and was terrified at the idea of speaking to a large audience. He was sweating and only managed to say, "Thank you all for coming here, and I would like to thank Mr. Dhole, who has helped me a lot in this case." A long pause. He did not find any further words to say. Everyone was quite, waiting for the main part of the speech apart from the 'Thank yous'. However, that main part never came out, and an awkward silence of 30 seconds followed. Rajiv couldn't say a single word, and finally, his judicial instincts kicked in. "I thank you all again for coming here, but a huge gathering outside the police station is a punishable offence, so, I request you all to please clear the area. Thank you again for coming here, in support for us." In any other scenario, the crowd could have taken an offence about this, but as of then, anything coming out of Rajiv's mouth was golden. The crowd understood Rajiv's camera shyness, laughed it off, and dispersed.

That night, Rajiv was drinking alone, in his home, to celebrate his victory. Often, when you are drinking alone and have no one to talk with, one goes soul searching. They try to figure out about themselves. From a bird's eye view, were they good or bad as a human being? What have they done wrong? How have they hurt others? What they have done good and all those spiritual dive. Rajiv was having one such trip. He felt bad that he had used his influences to ruin an academic year of the eleventh standard Dhruv. He suddenly realized that for his actions, Dhruv would have to answer throughout every job interview, why he had a year gap between boards of tenth and twelfth. He felt bad about it and cursed himself for it. After thinking about it for few minutes, he suddenly sat straight on his sofa. He thought about something and immediately dialed a number. He talked over phone for the next 5 minutes and then furiously called Saloni. Saloni was studying and took few minutes to answer to her Dad's call. “Saloni, you knew very well that I was going to pick you up exactly at 7.15 pm from the temple, which is near to your tuition centre. Then, what were you doing there, at the same time, with your boyfriend? That too, holding hands and kissing! You are a smart girl and would never play so lose and get caught. If you wanted to hide your boyfriend from me, you would not bring him to the place I was going to be and definitely not kiss him. Tell me what's going on, NOW!”

Rajiv ended up shouting at his daughter, so loud, that even his wife came out from the bedroom. Saloni got scared and was about to cry, but Rajiv caught hold of her and shook her to yield the truth from her. Her mother came running to take the side of her daughter, but Rajiv looked up at Devika and glared at her to tell her not to intervene. Devika didn't understand what it was about, but she trusted Rajiv's judgment and did not move a step closer. She became a spectator to the drama.

Saloni was a stubborn girl and kept quiet, but Rajiv's habit of homework before an interrogation gave him the leverage. Rajiv yelled, “I just now had a word with your ex-boyfriend Dhruv. He said that you proposed to him 2 weeks back, and you called him to the tuitions that day.”

Saloni looked up at Rajiv now, with fear. She was trapped. She looked back at her mother for help, but Devika and Rajiv had an understanding that none of them would take sides of their daughter during a session of stern parenting. Devika was panting. She wanted to rush and loosen Rajiv's grip on Saloni as she knew that it must be hurting her daughter, but she resisted her motherly instincts to become a better mother.

Rajiv roared again, "Look at me Saloni, look at me. Why did you do this? Tell me. Dhruv also told me that he did not want to kiss you, but you whispered to him for a goodbye kiss. Dhruv told you that it was a public place, but you dared him. Why?"

Devika was shaken. Her daughter asked a boy to kiss her, in public! But how did Rajiv know of it? She had many a questions but she knew that she should not interfere now. That would ruin the pressure that has built up.

Saloni again looked back at her mother with tears in her eyes. Devika's heart shattered to see tears in her daughter's eyes, but she did not come forward to help. Saloni knew that she was cornered, and the anger in her father's eyes scared her to death. She finally gave up. She started crying and said, "Dhruv is a bad boy, Dad; he ruined my best friend Dhriti's life. Dhriti and Dhruv were in a relation, and they got physical at Dhruv's place, when his parents were not home. After using her, Dhruv dumped her, and since then, Dhriti has been acting like a zombie. She has no feelings anymore; she does not talk or smile or laugh. She just keeps staring at everything. I could not see her like that, and I promised her that I will punish him. He deserved it. I knew that you would not help me if I ask you directly, but you will always protect me. Therefore, I became his girlfriend. That evening, I knew that you would come to pick me, and I called Dhruv so that you catch us kissing. I asked him to kiss me when I saw your car approaching. He hesitated, as it was a public place. I dared him to kiss me or break up with me. Finally, he kissed me, and you saw it. That's when I slapped him so that you think that he was forcing himself upon me. I had to do it Dad. Finally, Dhriti is smiling again, knowing that Dhruv has been punished."

Rajiv was dumbfounded and could not speak for a few moments. "Do you know what you have made me do? I ruined an academic year in his career and put a black spot in his resume. It is going to hurt him throughout his life. How dare you use me like that?" Rajiv raised his hands to slap her, but Devika came rushing, to the rescue and pulled her dear Saloni away. There was a limit to parenting, and both of them should stay within that limit. She said firmly, "I will deal with this, you do not get into it," and she took her away to another room.

Rajiv was still in rage and could not stop thinking about it. Soon, another thought grasped him. He immediately grabbed his phone and rang Mr Dhole. Mr. Dhole was used to late night calls. It was a professional hazard. As soon as Mr. Dhole answered the phone, Rajiv spilled, "Do we have Mr. Balaram Shetty's bank details?"

Mr. Dhole was startled. "Mr. Balaram Shetty's bank details! Sir, he is already dead. What can we do with his bank details?"

"I want Mr. Balaram Shetty's bank details by 9 am tomorrow morning; is that understood?"

Mr. Dhole knew that it would take him at least 10 am to get the reports, but he dared not say it and answered in the affirmative. But Rajiv did not stop. "The Shetty siblings told us, about the night of the murder, when Mr. Balaram Shetty declared his will. They told us that Mr. Balaram Shetty had mentioned that his lawyer would come the next day, but no lawyer came to Kunj Villa since then. Why?"

Mr. Dhole meekly said, "I don't know, sir."

"Get me his lawyer's number right now. I want to talk to him. Arrange for a conference call between me, you, and the lawyer, urgently."

Mr. Dhole looked at the time. It was 11 pm at night, he cursed Rajiv and his job silently, and said "I would have asked why do I need to do this, but I know you will not answer me now. Ok, sir, I am arranging for the conference call."

Five minutes later, they were having the conference call with Mr. Prasad, the family lawyer of Mr. Balaram Shetty.

"Mr. Prasad, I am sorry to call you this late, but it is about Mr. Balaram Shetty's death, and we need to talk with you urgently. Hope you do not mind."

"No not at all, tell me. How can I help?"

"The night Mr. Balaram died, he told everyone that you were supposed to come to Kunj Villa the next morning, to finalize Mr. Balaram's will. However, you did not come the next day!"

"What? I was not supposed to come the next day. Mr. Shetty never asked me to come, and what will are we talking about? He did not have any will, and neither did he ever discuss about a will with me."

Mr. Dhole could not shy away from the conversation. "But he had said to his children that he had a discussion with you for his will, and he even detailed what he was leaving for everyone."

"I am sorry, Inspector, but I was not informed about any will by Mr. Balaram Shetty. The last time I met with Mr. Balaram at his home was two days before his death. I did what he asked for, on the same day. I had no further plans to meet him anytime soon."

Rajiv asked, "What did he ask you to do?"

"He gave me a cheque of 60 lakh rupees in the name of a cancer research organization. I was surprised and asked him to rethink, as the amount was huge. However, he had already made up his mind. Then, he gave me 5 lakh rupees cash from the locker and asked me to deposit it to Hari's account. He even gave Hari's account number to me. I wanted to advice against the whole thing, but he was not willing to listen."

"By Hari, you mean the domestic help in Kunj Villa?"

"Yes, Mr. Rajiv."

"Ok, thanks, Mr. Prasad; thanks for your time."

CHAPTER 29

ArpitaTalukdar

♡ ◯ ∇ ⊓

8278 likes

ArpitaTalukdar Rajiv Bakshi, you are my real life hero. You are the best police officer in India and you have stolen my heart, I LOVE YOU Rajiv Bakshi.

P.S – Please do not show this to Mrs. Bakshi ;)

#mycrush #ilovehim #nationalhero #JusticeServed

View all 1781 comments

55 MINUTES AGO

Next day, Rajiv and Mr. Dhole were going through Mr. Balaram's bank statement. While going through it, Rajiv saw that 60 lakh rupees had already been debited to the cancer research organization. After that cheque had passed, Mr. Balaram Shetty had INR 37, 54, 980 left in his account. Rajiv drilled further down and marked an Amazon transaction. He ordered Mr. Dhole to get the details of it immediately. Few minutes later, Mr. Dhole confirmed that the Amazon transaction in Mr. Balaram's account was to buy an industrial glue. Rajiv put his hands in his forehead and stared at the table in despair. Mr. Dhole still did not understand the reason for Rajiv's frustration. "What is the problem with this Sir?"

"Mr. Balaram threatened his sons and daughter that he will give away 60 lakh rupees to charity and wrote a cheque, enacting a drama, whereas his account did not have that much money, and he had already deposited that amount to the charity by then. He even deposited five lakh rupees to Hari's account. Therefore, the will he threatened to the family members was one he had already implemented it, two days before his birthday. As per the will he discussed that night, the rest of his properties were supposed to be distributed more or less evenly among his children which is what would happen now too, as there are no official will. Therefore, the will he detailed that night, was a threat to his children, so that they would become the prime suspect of his murder. The signing of that cheque meant that the siblings had to act fast."

Mr. Dhole responded, "But Mr. Vicky, Mrs. Pubali, and Mrs. Ronit murdered him that night, and we have arrested them on those charges too."

"If Mr. Balaram brought the Industrial glue that was used to lock the doors from the inside, it changes the whole story. It means that Mr. Ronit did not use the glue to lock the doors from the inside. The glue could not be used by Mr. Balaram himself, as he was already dead, so he must have used an accomplice to apply the glue to the door. The only person in Kunj Villa, who would help Mr. Balaram is his loyal servant, Hari. Only Hari could have applied the glue to the door."

Mr. Dhole still did not get it, "But why Sir? Why would Hari do it?"

"I will tell you a story; let's see if that helps you see from my point of view. My daughter Saloni wanted to punish a boy because the boy used a friend of hers for physical pleasures and then dumped her friend. Saloni knew she was powerless against the boy, so she tricked me into punishing that boy. Similarly, Mr. Balaram knew that Mr. Ronit was guilty of murdering his wife, Mrs. Sabitri, who Mr. Balaram loved as his own daughter. Mr. Balaram knew that Mrs. Pubali was wrong to harass her husband and his family in this divorce case. She was just greedy for the alimony and ruining other's life and social image for her own financial gain. Mr. Balaram also knew that Mr. Vicky was a rapist, and he had raped their previous maid. Mr. Balaram could not do anything when Mr. Vicky was harassing his own sister-in-law, Mrs. Sabitri. Mr. Balaram lived with this guilt, but the same thing was happening again. Mr. Balaram knew that his eldest son has set his lusty eyes on Mr. Balaram's eldest daughter-in-law, Mrs. Aparjita. This time, he could not afford to let it happen and ignore it; so, he had to do something to stop it. Mr. Balaram must have blamed himself for the poor upbringing of his children, which made them grow up to be monsters. He was too old to do anything about it, but he would not sit quite. Therefore, he made the ultimate sacrifice. He plotted his own murder and planted evidence so that Mr. Vicky. Mrs. Pubali, and Mr. Ronit can be charged of murder, and finally, Indian law can punish them. Not for their original sins but a much graver sin. After all, he always said that justice must prevail, at any cost. He paid the highest price for justice. The perfect Queen sacrifice and Check Mate move."

"But sir, we have evidence."

"I don't know if I am right, it is my presumption, but let's go over them again. Let's just suppose that the siblings are telling the truth, and also let's suppose that my theory is true. Mr. Balaram Shetty arranged for the evidence, using Hari. Let's go over them, one by one."

"Ok, sir, first, Mr. Vicky. We have the cigarette bud and his fingerprints on the pillow cover."

"That's easy. Hari can arrange for both of them. Just get a smoked cigarette bud from Mr. Vicky's room and interchange Mr. Vicky and Mr. Balaram's pillow covers, one day before the murder. He only needs to use gloves while doing this."

"But Sir, the autopsy report says that Mr. Balaram was suffocated; then who suffocated him?"

"I think Mr. Balaram instructed Hari to suffocate him while he was sleeping. Painless death. I am sure Hari would have strongly denied first, but Mr. Balaram must have somehow convinced Hari that this was for the greater good, and this was the painless death he had wished for. I am sure that is why he took the sleeping pills also. He would not have even felt a bit of pain while dying. Of course, getting a sleeping pill from Mrs. Pubali was also a ploy to make sure Mrs. Pubali falls into the trap, as the chemical would show up in the autopsy report. Hari can easily access the bottle of Mrs. Pubali's sleeping pills and take 14 sleeping pills from it. I am sure that, once Mrs. Pubali gave her Dad a sleeping pill and left the room, Mrs. Balaram would have taken the extra 14 sleeping pills which were fetched by Hari."

"What about the knife?"

"That must have been done well beyond 3 am. By that time, Hari knew that Mr. Balaram was already dead. Hari would only be stabbing a dead body. We know that Mr. Ronit was hiding the knife in his room initially. Hari regularly cleaned his room, and so he must have known all along, where it was. Mr. Balaram Shetty knew that Mr. Ronit used that knife to kill his wife and stage it as a suicide. At that time, Mr. Balaram Shetty might have even supported his son by ensuring a loose investigation, but he regretted it. Now that he was willing to set some old wrongs right, he used that knife to trap his son. That way, even Mrs. Sabitri would get justice. We must remember that Mr. Balaram Shetty was fanatical about justice. Hari only had to get that knife and use that knife to stab Mr. Balaram's already lifeless corpse. Then he would wash the knife and put it in the original hiding spot in Mr. Ronit's room. If you remember, Mr. Ronit had confirmed that he was stoned that night and he would not have noticed any of it. The next day, before the rooms were going to be searched, Mr. Ronit hid the same knife in the garden, in fears of connection to Mrs. Sabitri's murder."

"But why then lock the doors from the inside? If the doors were open, it would have been easier for us to suspect that one of the children had murdered Mr. Balaram."

"The answer to that lies in Mr. Balaram's library. A man is what kind of books he reads. Mr. Balaram's mini library is decked with detective books. Any crime reader loves drama and the complexity of the crime and the struggles to solve the murder case. No reader likes a murder story which points to the murderer on the first day of the investigation. This was Mr. Balaram's chance to stage the story as he wanted it. The detective in his story has to be smart to find the murderer. He wasn't going to hand his children on a plate to the detective. So, he arranged for the ventilator shaft to be removed from his washroom. This adds the element of external influence to the list of suspects to tread through. Then he did a classic. Murder behind locked doors, how did the murderer escape? It's his story, and he wrote it damn well."

"So, you are saying the children did not have anything to do with Mr. Balaram's murder? Hari murdered him on his instructions and glued the door on his way out?"

"I am saying that the children were the reason this murder was staged, but they did not murder their father. Mr. Balaram Shetty enacted the drama of the will declaration to set the stage so that his heirs come to his room on the night he was going to kill himself."

"Then how do we prove the truth? We do not have any evidence!"

Rajiv had a wicked but satisfying smile on his face. He took a pause, walked towards the window and said, "Who said anything about proving the truth? We don't even know which of our theories is true and which is not. If this theory is true, then this is a former High Court Judge's final and greatest justice sentence. As usual, we will follow the judge's orders," Rajiv ended the sentence with a blink and a wide smile.

"Then what do we do, sir?"

"You file the charge sheet for Mr. Vicky, Mrs. Pubali, and Mr. Ronit. File it such that there are no loopholes by which these bastards can avoid a sentence. Meanwhile, let me see how I can fix my daughter's fraud boyfriend's situation. I will ensure that he does not miss an academic year, but also, I need to teach him a lesson. No one gets away after kissing my daughter."

The two shared a good laugh and went their separate ways to respective duties.

Arvind Chatterjee

1 h

@Bangalore Policeand **@Rajiv Bakshi**, you 2 are fantastic. Great work and effort to solve this heinous crime. That closed door part, it fooled me but you guys still caught the murderers. Well done man.

#JusticeServed #BangalorePoliceisgreat

#RajivBakshiNationalHero

4k Likes 376 Comments 117 Shares

------- THE END ------

www.ingramcontent.com/pod-product-compliance
Ingram Content Group UK Ltd.
Pitfield, Milton Keynes, MK11 3LW, UK
UKHW042018190726
13854UKWH00005B/2345